PRAISE FOR
ANNABELLE DIXON COZY MYSTERY
SERIES

"Absolutely wonderful!!"

"Delightful."

"I read it that night, and it was GREAT!"

"I couldn't put it down!"

"4 thumbs up!!!"

"It kept me up until 3am. I love it."

"As a former village vicar this ticks the box for me."

"This series keeps getting better and better."

"Annabelle, with her great intuition, caring personality, yet
imperfect judgement, is a wonderful main character."

"It's fun to grab a cup of tea and pretend I'm sitting in the
vicarage discussing the latest mysteries with Annabelle
whilst she polishes off the last of the cupcakes."

"Great book - love Reverend Annabelle Dixon and can't
wait to read more of her books."

"Annabelle reminds me of Agatha Christie's Miss Marple."

"A perfect weekend read."

"I LOVE ANNABELLE!"

"A wonderful read, delightful characters and if that's not

enough the sinfully delicious recipes will have you coming back for more."

"This cozy series is a riot!"

DEATH AT THE CAFÉ

BOOKS IN THE REVEREND ANNABELLE DIXON SERIES

Chaos in Cambridge (Prequel)

Death at the Café

Murder at the Mansion

Body in the Woods

Grave in the Garage

Horror in the Highlands

Killer at the Cult

Fireworks in France

Witches at the Wedding

COLLECTIONS

Books 1-4

Death at the Café

Murder at the Mansion

Body in the Woods

Grave in the Garage

Books 5-7

Horror in the Highlands

Killer at the Cult

Fireworks in France

DEATH AT THE CAFÉ

ALISON GOLDEN

JAMIE VOUGEOT

Published by Mesa Verde Publishing
P.O. Box 1002
San Carlos, CA 94070

ISBN: 978-1517022167

"Books are engines of change, windows on the world, and lighthouses erected in the sea of time. They are companions, teachers, magicians, bankers of the treasures of the mind. Books are humanity in print."
- Barbara Tuchman -

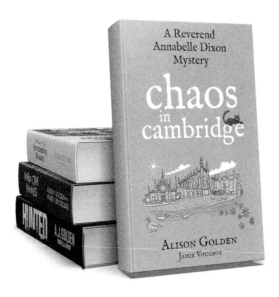

"Your emails seem to come on days when I need to read them because they are so upbeat."
- Linda W -

For a limited time, you can get the first books in each of my series - *Chaos in Cambridge, Hunted* (exclusively for subscribers - not available anywhere else), *The Case of the Screaming Beauty, and Mardi Gras Madness* - plus updates about new releases, promotions, and other Insider exclusives, by signing up for my mailing list at:

https://www.alisongolden.com/annabelle

NOTE FROM THE AUTHOR

The events in this book take place a few years before *Murder at the Mansion*, the next in the Reverend Annabelle Dixon series of cozy mysteries. It is set in London.

Death at the Café and others in the series are complete mysteries. They can be read and enjoyed in any order. I've made sure not to include any spoilers for those of you who are new to the characters. Any existing fans of Annabelle's escapades will still find plenty of fresh action and mystery, as well as a little background detail on some of the major players in the Reverend Annabelle universe. All in all, there is something for everyone.

You can get the prequel to this series, *Chaos in Cambridge*, exclusively for my newsletter readers and not available anywhere else, by signing up here: https://dl.book funnel.com/2hfrj6g1cl

I had an absolute blast creating this book – I hope you have a blast reading it too.

Alison Golden

CHAPTER ONE

NOTHING BROUGHT REVEREND Annabelle closer to blasphemy than using the London public transport system during rush hour. Since being ordained and sent to St. Clement's church, an impressive, centuries-old building among the tower blocks and new builds of London's East End, Annabelle had been tested many times. She had come across virtually every sin known to man, counselled wayward youths, presided over family disputes, heard astonishingly sad tales from the homeless, and still retained her solid, optimistic dependability through it all. None of these challenges made her blood boil, and her round, soft face curl up into a mixture of disgust, frustration, and exasperation. Yet sitting on the number forty-three bus to Islington, as it moved along at a snail's pace, was almost enough to make her take her beloved Lord's name in vain.

On this occasion, she had nabbed her favourite seat: top deck, front left. It gave her a perfect view of the unique streets London offered and the even more varied types of people. Today, however, her viewpoint afforded her only a teeth-clenchingly irritating perspective of a traffic jam that extended as far as the eye could see down Upper Street.

"I know I shouldn't," she muttered on the relatively empty bus, "but if this doesn't deserve a cherry-topped cupcake, then I don't know what does."

The thought of rewarding her patience with what she loved almost as much as her vocation—cake—settled Annabelle's nerves for a full twenty minutes, during which the bus trundled in fits and starts along another half-mile stretch.

Assigning Annabelle, fresh from her days studying theology at Cambridge University, to the tough, inner-city borough of Hackney had presented her with what had been an almost literal baptism of fire. She had arrived in the summer, during a few weeks when the British sun combined with the squelching heat of a city constantly bustling and moving. It was a time of drinking and frivolity for some, heightened tension for others. A spell during which bored youths found their idle hands easily occupied with the devil's work. An interval when the good relax and the bad run riot.

Annabelle had grown up in East London, but for her first appointment as a vicar, her preference had been for a peaceful, rural village somewhere. A place in which she could indulge her love of nature, and conduct her Holy business in the gentle, caring manner she preferred. "Gentle" and "caring," however, were two words rarely used to describe London. Annabelle had mildly protested her city assignment. But after a long talk to the archbishop who explained the extreme shortage of candidates both capable and willing to take on the challenge of an inner-city church, she agreed to take up the position and set about her task with enthusiasm.

Father John Wilkins of neighbouring St. Leonard's church had been charged with easing Annabelle into the complex role. He had been a priest for over thirty years, and for the vast majority of that time had worked in London's poorest, toughest neighbourhoods. The Anglican Church was far less popular in London than it was in rural England, largely due to the city's disparate mix of peoples and creeds. Father John's congregation was mostly made up of especially devout immigrants from Africa and South America, many of whom were not even Anglican but simply lived nearby. The only time St. Leonard's had ever been full was on a particularly mild Christmas Eve.

But despite low attendance at services, London's churches played pivotal roles in their local communities. With plenty of people in need, they were hubs of charity and community support. Fundraising events, providing food and shelter for London's large homeless population, caring for the elderly, and engaging troubled youths were the churches' stock in trade, not to mention they provided both spiritual and emotional support for the many deaths and family tragedies that occurred.

The stress of it all had turned Father John's wiry beard a speckled grey, and though he knew his work was important and worthwhile, he had been pushed to breaking point on more than one occasion. Upon her arrival, he had taken one look at Annabelle's breezy manner and fresh-faced, open smile and assumed that her appointment was a case of negligence, desperation, or a sick prank.

"She's utterly delightful," Father John sighed on the phone to the archbishop, "and extremely nice. But 'delightful' and 'nice' are not what's required in a London church. This is a part of the world where faith is stretched to its very limits, where strong leadership goes further than gentle guidance. We struggle to capture people's attention, Archbishop, let alone their hearts. Our drug rehabilitation programs have more members than our congregations."

"Give her a chance, Father," the archbishop replied softly. "Don't underestimate her. She grew up in East London, you know."

"Well, I grew up in Westminster, but that doesn't mean I've had tea with the Queen!"

Merely a week into Annabelle's assignment, however, Father John's misgivings proved unfounded. Annabelle's bumbling, naïve manner was just that—a manner. Father John observed closely as Annabelle's strength, faith, and intelligence were consistently tested by the urban issues of her flock. He noted that she passed with flying colours.

Whether she was dealing with a hardened criminal fresh out of prison and already succumbing to old temptations, or a single mother of three struggling to find some composure and faith in the face of her daily troubles, Annabelle was always there to help. With good humour and optimism, she never turned down a request for assistance, no matter how large or small it was.

When Father John visited Annabelle a month after the start of her placement to check on a highly successful gardening project she had started for troubled youth, he shook his head in amazement "Is that Denton? By the rose bushes? I've been trying to get him to visit me for a year now, and all he does is ignore me. You should hear what he says when his parole officer suggests it," he said.

"Oh, Denton is wonderful!" Annabelle cried. "Fantastic with his hands. He has a devilish sense of humour—when it's properly directed. Did you know that he plays drums?"

"No, I didn't know that. He never told me," Father John said, giving Annabelle an appreciative smile. "I must say,

Reverend, I seem to have misjudged you dreadfully. And I apologise."

"Oh, Father," Annabelle chuckled, "it's perfectly understandable. You have only the best interests of the community at heart. Let's leave judgement for Him and Him alone. The only thing we're meant to judge is cake contests, in my opinion. Mind those thorns, Denton! Roses tend to fight back if you treat them roughly!"

CHAPTER TWO

PROGRESS IN THE service of the Lord was not matched by that of the London Bus Network on this occasion, however. The bus rolled forwards and stopped, mere feet away from where it had started. Annabelle stood up to get a better view of the road ahead and scanned the long snake of traffic that extended in front of, and behind the bus. She exchanged a shrug with a kindly-looking Jamaican, his grey curls tucked underneath his porkpie hat.

"Fiddlesticks," she uttered, too exasperated to contain herself. "I'm supposed to meet someone, an old friend."

"Aye," the Jamaican man replied in his heavily accented English. "The Lord moves in mysterious ways."

"Well, at least He moves, unlike this bus," Annabelle replied, sitting back down and clasping her hands.

After another ten minutes, the bus rolled forwards a little further, dejectedly opening its doors a full twenty yards ahead of a stop. Annabelle decided to walk the rest of her journey and stepped off the bus into a crowd of people who all wore the same downtrodden expression of defeat.

Foregoing her usual laid-back, serene pace for one that would minimise the lateness of her meeting with her friend, Annabelle marched down the high street, her cassock flowing behind her, resolute about the cherry-topped cupcake she was planning on eating. She also considered the benefits of buying a bicycle. She had been looking forward to tea with Mary. It was to be the last time they would meet for a very long time.

Annabelle and Mary had been friends since they were babies. Mary had been born in the same year as Annabelle, in the back seat of the cab Annabelle's father drove for a living. With Mary's mother in an advanced stage of labour and having recently witnessed the birth of his own daughter, Annabelle's father was all too aware of how impossible it would be to get Mary's mother to the hospital on time. He had pulled up outside the nearest grocery store, and with the help of the shop owner who provided towels and water, he had delivered Mary himself. With Mary's parents feeling deeply indebted to Annabelle's father for the successful birth of their child, the families—and thus the children—became lifelong friends.

In some ways, Mary and Annabelle were strikingly different. Annabelle was tall and sturdy with an ever-present smile on her face. Mary was small and slim. She was less robust than Annabelle and had a resting facial expression that was more circumspect. It was, however, Annabelle's enthusiasm and Mary's nose for adventure that caused the two girls to become almost inseparable until Annabelle left London to study at Cambridge University and Mary went to train as a nurse.

Mary was an interesting character. Peculiar occurrences followed her around. Although she was slight, her five-foot-three looking even smaller next to Annabelle's towering frame, she had a habit of being at the centre of things. Her first day at school ended prematurely when an administrative error had her registered as a teacher. She was given her own classroom until the mistake was discovered. Years later, she passed her driving test with full marks, less for her ability to follow the Highway Code and more for the expert precision with which she avoided an escaped bull that found itself on the M25. Even the simple purchase of a second-hand coat turned into an event when Mary found plans for an undiscovered portion of London's underground tunnels sewn into the seams.

One day whilst completing her nursing training, Mary attended a routine lecture on hospital procedures only to find she had stumbled into a talk given by an order of nuns working in West Africa. Instead of discreetly leaving to double-check her planner, Mary stayed to listen. The talk of exotic climates, dangerous but fulfilling work, and the nuns' devotion to their mission captivated her. Mary had been raised a strict Catholic, and just minutes after the talk had ended, she made up her mind—she would become a nun and go to West Africa. In time, she became Sister Mary and had performed her ministries in Africa for a few years now. She was in London for a visit and had contacted Annabelle to suggest tea.

As Annabelle drew closer to the café where Mary requested they meet, she spied a gathering crowd of onlookers. She felt her heart skip. "Oh dear, Mary," she whispered, "what on earth has happened this time?"

"Excuse me," Annabelle called, as she made her way through the crowd. The bystanders stood aside for her, partly because of the authority her cassock conveyed and partly because Annabelle was taller than most of them. "Vicar coming through!" she trilled.

When she broke through to the space inside the circle of gawkers, Annabelle came to an abrupt halt. Stunned by the scene before her, her hand reflexively rose to her mouth. She gasped. A young woman was sprawled next to an outside table, a waiter crouched beside her barking out instructions for the crowd to stay back.

The woman on the ground was young and beautiful. Her golden-blonde hair splayed out on the dirty pavement. She wore a simple but well-fitting pair of jeans and an elegant jacket. Her outfit gave her the appearance of a trendy woman-about-town were it not for the fact that she lay on the grey concrete. Her pallor was pale, her lips were still pink, but her light-blue eyes were lifeless and dull. With disinterest, she gazed into the sky far above her as if witnessing the flight of her soul.

CHAPTER THREE

TWO GREEN-SUITED paramedics burst through the crowd with the swift and brutal air of a job done a thousand times. They dropped their bags beside the woman's dead body and went to work, talking with the waiter who spoke continuously whilst shaking his head in disbelief.

Annabelle peeled her eyes from the scene and noticed Mary. Her friend wore her civvies not her nun's habit, and stood on the other side of the crowd. Her hand was over her mouth, and she visibly shook.

Mary had been in West Africa. She had studied nursing. When it came to tragedy, she had seen it all. It would take something unusually shocking for Mary to look so shaken. Annabelle's instincts told her something stranger than a straightforward death had occurred. Annabelle marched over to her friend. Mary's eyes were transfixed by the woman's dead body. She didn't notice Annabelle until the vicar grasped the nun in her arms and hugged her gently.

"Mary! Are you okay?"

"Oh, Annabelle," Mary said, allowing herself to be enveloped by her friend.

Annabelle patted Mary's back until she had stopped shaking. She pulled away and looked Mary in the eye. "What on earth happened?" Annabelle said. She took Mary's arm and led her away from the crowd.

"It was awful, Annabelle," Mary said, sniffing. "She . . . the dead woman . . . she walked up to me. And then she just dropped to her knees and fell over. She twitched a bit and then seconds later, she stopped moving. I don't know what happened, Annabelle. I really don't."

"She walked up to you?" Annabelle said, pulling an ever-handy pack of tissues from her pocket and handing one to Mary. "You knew her?"

"No," Mary said, before blowing her nose into the tissue, "but I was to meet someone here, just before you came."

"Who?"

Mary gave her nose one last blow before speaking. "I've been in London for a month now. I've been looking for funding. As hard as we work, the hospitals in Africa simply can't cope without enormous amounts of money. I was to meet someone here who might have been able to help us."

"The dead woman?"

Mary shook her head, too overwhelmed by the situation to think properly. "I don't know. I don't believe so. We'd only spoken over the phone, but I'm sure the person I spoke to was much older."

Officious shouts to clear the pavement caught their attention. Annabelle looked away from Mary's small, pretty face to see police officers ushering onlookers away.

"Sorry, ladies," a nearby officer said, "would you mind

moving just a little further down the road? We're going to have to tape the entire area. Thank you."

"Officer," Annabelle called before he could turn away, "this woman saw the death." The policeman turned back and cast his eyes over Mary who managed a mild nod from behind her scrunched-up tissue.

"Detective Inspector!" he bawled. He pointed at Mary. "Someone here you need to speak to." Seconds later, the two women found themselves joined by a short, bulky man. He resembled an English bulldog.

"Detective Inspector Cutcliffe," he said as if even pronouns were a waste of time. He was unshaven and there was mud around the soles of his shoes.

Everything about DI Cutcliffe was rough. Everything from the heavy jacket he wore to his angular, uncompromising jawline. He seemed to exist in a shroud of bad humour. There was a pool running in his police branch to see who could make him laugh. It had run to hundreds of pounds, and there still wasn't a winner.

His fellow officers may have mocked Cutcliffe but never to his face. The DI was the kind of detective who could do damage with a look. He was the butt of many private jokes but the public recipient of none. He also happened to be one of the most respected detectives in London. Every officer in the capital had heard of him. He asked more questions than a game show host, and he hadn't lost a case since 1982.

"Name?" he growled, his notebook and pen seemingly materialising from nowhere into his hand.

"Sister Mary Willis."

"And I'm Reverend Annabelle Dixon."

DI Cutcliffe's eyes darted between the two women.

"Anglican?" he said, spearing the word in Annabelle's direction, like a bayonet.

"Yes."

"And you're Catholic?" he said, pointing his pen at Mary.

"Yes."

"How do you know each other?"

"We've been friends since . . . well, forever," Annabelle said, looking at Mary who confirmed Annabelle's words with a vehement nod.

DI Cutcliffe shrugged away this line of inquiry before starting a fresh one. "So you saw what happened?"

"Yes," Mary said.

"Describe exactly how it went."

"Yes. I mean, no. I mean, yes, I'll describe it," Mary stammered, finding the detective's flinty tone unnerving. "I was waiting to meet someone. Here, at the café."

"The Reverend?"

"Yes, but not her. Before her, someone else. Someone I'd never met before."

CHAPTER FOUR

THE DETECTIVE INSPECTOR fixed Mary with a penetrating glare. "You were due to meet someone here?"

"Yes. Someone interested in funding a hospital in Africa."

"The dead woman was interested in funding a hospital in Africa?"

"No, not her. At least, I don't think it was her. I'd only spoken to my contact on the phone. I'm fairly certain it wasn't the woman . . . over there." Mary nodded at the body on the ground. "The person I was meeting was much older, I'm sure." The detective nodded.

"I noticed the woman, the dead one," Mary continued, "walking towards me. She was extremely close, barely a foot away. She seemed fine. Then . . ." Mary began shaking again, losing her composure as she relived the memory. "Sorry," she said. "Then she, the woman, collapsed. Flat on the ground. As you see her now."

"So she was looking at you. But you don't think she was the person you were going to meet?"

"No," said Mary. "I don't think so."

"But she was looking at you."

"Yes . . . no . . . oh, I can't be sure, but I think so. Maybe I'm wrong. It was all so . . . fast. I thought maybe she had mistaken me for someone else, or that she was a waitress, or wanted to ask for directions . . . I don't know, Detective Inspector, I'm sorry. "

"I see," Cutcliffe said, scribbling something down so furiously Annabelle was sure he would rip the paper in his notebook. "So she may or may not have been the person you were due to meet. She walked up to you and collapsed. Then what happened?"

"I screamed and jumped out of my chair. The waiter came over and checked on her. I'm a nurse so I tried to help, but then . . . a doctor came."

DI Cutcliffe raised his eyebrows ever so slightly. On a face more expressive, the gesture would have barely been noticeable. On Cutcliffe, the effect was amplified.

"You mean the paramedics?"

"No, not the paramedics. When the woman collapsed, people on the street turned to see what was going on. This man came from the other side of the road and pushed through the crowd. He said he was a doctor. He kneeled over the woman and checked her pulse, then . . . I'm so sorry. I don't know what happened. I was so shaken. I've seen some things, but this was so unexpected."

"Where is this doctor now?"

Mary looked around for a full five seconds. "I don't know. He must have left. When I saw him tending to the woman, I looked away, and when I looked back, he had disappeared."

"Describe him for me."

Mary stared off into space for a while, squinting as if it

would help her see further into her own memory. "It's diffi-cult. I didn't really see his face. He dressed very strikingly though. He wore a dark brown suit. Tweed, perhaps. It looked very expensive. A waistcoat too. Brown leather shoes."

DI Cutcliffe let out a barely perceptible sigh. "If I get a sketch artist, do you think you could describe him?"

Mary winced. "I could try, but I'm sorry, I really doubt it. It's as if the more I try to remember him, the more I struggle..."

"Relax. It will come to you."

"But it's the strangest thing. At the time I thought I had seen him clearly, but now for the life of me, I can't recall him."

"You say he said he was a doctor. Was there any kind of an accent? What did he sound like?"

Mary bit her lip and looked away again. "Actually, I didn't notice an accent. He sounded . . . like a typical Londoner, I suppose. If there is such a thing."

Cutcliffe stared at Mary with eyes that seemed to exca-vate her soul, sizing up whether the small woman was hiding something. After a few seconds of this intense glare, he flipped to a blank page in his notebook, handed it to Mary along with a pen, and said: "Write down your tele-phone number and contact details." Mary obliged, quickly scribbling her details down on the notepad.

"Inspector," Annabelle said, seizing the moment, "does this mean we can go? Sister Mary seems incredibly shaken, and I'd like to take her somewhere she can gather herself."

The detective's small, dark eyes shifted to Annabelle's wide, bright ones. They darted to her clerical collar. He nodded as if he were allowing her a great privilege. "You can go, but don't leave the city. I may need more information about this person you were meeting, as well as this *doctor*."

Mary handed back the inspector's notebook, and he gave the two women his card in exchange.

"If you remember anything, and I mean anything, call me." Cutcliffe turned his penetrating gaze on Annabelle. "I'm always willing to give the benefit of the doubt to Holy men—or women. Even though it's been known to backfire in the past. Good day to you."

Annabelle and Mary exchanged frightened glances as the inspector turned on his heel. He was already barking out instructions to his officers. Annabelle found herself almost as shaken as her friend.

"Whatever could that be about?" she said, careful that her words couldn't be overheard by any of the police at the scene. "Come on, Mary, let's leave. We'll go somewhere quiet and have a nice cup of tea and a slice of cake." Mary nodded. She allowed Annabelle to take her by the arm and guide her down the street.

"Annabelle," Mary said, in her soft voice, "could I trouble you for another tissue?"

"Of course," Annabelle replied, fishing around for the packet in her cassock skirt. "Take the lot. You need them more than I do." She handed Mary the tissues.

"Thank you," the nun said, pulling a tissue out and putting the packet into her pocket. "Oh!" she cried suddenly. Mary whipped her hand out as if a mouse had been waiting to bite her finger. Clutched between her thumb and forefinger was a slip of paper.

"I completely forgot!" Mary exclaimed. "The woman who died. Before she collapsed—before she fell completely to the floor—she handed me this." Mary looked at the ruled piece of paper in her hand. It was folded neatly in four.

Annabelle's hands smacked her cheeks in surprise. She moved her lips silently as if unable to think of what to say. "Are you sure?" was the only thing that came to mind.

"Yes! I completely forgot in all the fuss. She had this note in her hand and reached out to me. I took it, and she fell. It was almost automatic of me. I was so focused on her eyes. The life was visibly leaving them . . ."

"Well, what does the note say?!" Annabelle said.

"I don't know," Mary shrugged, her friend's excitement confusing her. "I didn't have time to look at it."

"Well, read it!" Annabelle nearly screamed.

Mary stared at the slip of lined notepaper as if it were a fragile explosive. Carefully, she reached a finger into the crease and unfolded it. Annabelle watched wide-eyed and open-mouthed, her heart thumping.

Mary studied the contents for half a second, then gasped, her hand instinctively covering her mouth. In her shock, Mary dropped the paper. It floated to the ground.

With cat-like reflexes, Annabelle reached down to pick it up. "It says 'Teresa is in danger.' And then there's a number." Annabelle looked at Mary who was still clutching her hand to her mouth.

"Teresa is the name of the woman I was supposed to meet!" Mary cried. "What could it mean?"

Annabelle looked at the note as if the answer might appear on it. "Quick, let's go back and tell the inspector," Annabelle said.

The two women ran back the way they had come. They arrived at the café just in time to see the inspector pulling away from the kurb in his unmarked car, a police officer controlling traffic to allow Cutcliffe a route through the heavily trafficked lanes. They watched his car weave through the stationary vehicles and speed off down an empty side street.

"Fiddlesticks!" Annabelle cried out.

"What should we do now?" Mary said.

Annabelle scanned the road, then marched over to a red phone box.

"Are you going to call him?" Mary said as she struggled to keep up.

"No," Annabelle replied, determination clear in her voice, "I'm going to call the number on the note."

Mary's voice rose a full octave. "But Annabelle! We don't know what's going on! We should call the police."

"You're right, and there will be plenty of time for that. But the victim handed this note to you. Why did she do that? Why did she not go to the police directly? She must have had a good reason. We should find out what it was."

"I suppose you're right," Mary admitted.

"Look, we'll just check, and then if we need the police, we'll hand this to DI Cutcliffe immediately."

CHAPTER FIVE

ANNABELLE LISTENED INTENTLY to the phone ringing at the other end of the line. As she concentrated on the sound, she shifted her weight anxiously from one foot to the other. Mary stood a few feet away, glancing from side to side and up and down the busy street as if she were a lookout. It felt much like one of the many adventures they had enjoyed together as children. Perhaps it was the fact that they had not spoken for such a long time, the pair of them busy with their adult lives, but suddenly, it felt that they were reprising the well-worn roles of their youth; Annabelle taking the initiative, and Mary providing a willing, inventive counterfoil. The stakes this time around, however, felt a lot more dangerous than the risk of having their pocket money confiscated.

The ringing on the other end of the line stopped. Annabelle waved gleefully at Mary.

"Hello?" came a scratchy but warm voice on the other end of the line.

"Oh, ah . . . hello! Ah . . . is this Teresa?"

"Yes, I'm Teresa," came the cautious reply. "Who is this?"

"Ah, this is Reverend Annabelle Dixon. I have with me, Sister Mary Willis. I believe you know her."

"Yes, indeed I do," the woman replied, her voice hardening. Annabelle could hear the tension in her voice.

"Ah, well . . ." Annabelle stumbled over her words, wondering what she should say. She looked at Mary for a cue, but her friend's open-mouthed, wide-eyed expression provided her with none. "Well, ah . . . we received a message that suggested you may be in danger. We'd like to visit you as soon as possible. To make sure you're alright."

"Really? I see," Teresa said, her voice still wary. After a brief pause, she continued. "Well, that would probably be alright. I am at home. My address is 52 Glentworth Street. Head directly north from Baker Street station. My flat is on the second floor."

Annabelle nodded as Teresa spoke. "Thank you. We'll be there as quickly as possible. But please, be careful in the meantime."

"Goodbye," Teresa said after a second's hesitation. Annabelle slammed the receiver down and turned to Mary, her face alight.

"So? What did she say?" Mary asked, her large, round eyes urging Annabelle for information.

"It was a bit strange," Annabelle said, patting her hair. "She didn't seem fazed in the least by the idea that she might be in danger, nor did she make any mention of the meeting with you. If the idea weren't so outrageous, I'd say she was suspicious of *me*. Did she sound guarded when you spoke to her?"

Mary pursed her lips as she thought. "No, not at all. From our conversations—though they were few—she seemed a typical older lady. Warm, gentle, caring. A little humorous, even."

Annabelle pitched her shoulders back and stood fully upright like she often did when making an important decision. "Then we should make haste because something is up. Let's find out what it is." And with those words, Annabelle began to march to the nearest tube station, Sister Mary fluttering behind her like a pony-tailed butterfly.

The two women pushed through the turnstiles along with other London Underground travellers. They trotted down the many flights of stairs and reached the platform just as a train barrelled out from a dark tunnel. They hopped on. Annabelle threw herself onto her seat as if it were a comfy couch whilst Sister Mary sat down delicately like she was attending a polite afternoon tea.

"When I'm in Africa, I do so miss riding the tube," Mary said, displaying the unbridled optimism that was typical of her, despite it being barely an hour since a woman had dropped dead at her feet.

"If it were up to me, I'd happily give the complete transport system away," Annabelle replied, gently kicking an empty bottle that had rolled against her foot.

Mary giggled at Annabelle's grumbling. "How would you travel around London?"

Annabelle shrugged. "I'm beginning to think the best thing to do is to stay at home!"

Mary laughed again before pursed lips replaced her smile. "I am terribly sorry for all this fuss, Annabelle. It's such a shame that instead of catching up as we intended, we're going who-knows-where for what seems like a worrying, perhaps dangerous purpose."

"Oh, tosh," replied Annabelle. "It's fine. I'm sure this is all perfectly reasonable and will be clarified as soon as we have a chat and a cup of tea with this Teresa. Perhaps you'll even get to finalise your funding."

"That would be a wonderful outcome, for sure," Mary said.

"Come on, we have to change trains here."

"Where are we going?"

"Baker Street."

"Home of Sherlock Holmes," Mary added, a hint of amusement returning to her voice.

"Perhaps he can help us with this confounding turn of events!"

They got off the train, navigated the tunnels and escalators that led them to the Metropolitan line, and waited patiently on the platform.

"Do you remember the time that we went to a Halloween party," Mary began, after a moment's thought. "You as Sherlock Holmes and me as Jack the Ripper?"

"Of course!" Annabelle said, looking happily into the distance as she brought the memory to mind. "I had rather hoped you would go as Dr. Watson, though."

"That would have been ever so boring," Mary said. "So predictable. And you took things entirely too seriously."

"I did not!"

"You did!" responded Mary. "You spent the entire evening—both the trick-or-treating and the party afterwards —staring suspiciously at people over your plastic bubble pipe, trying to deduce who had committed the crime, the crime in question being the taking of a bite from your Halloween cupcake."

Annabelle laughed. "Well, perhaps I was a little overzealous. Your cousin, Josh, was there. I've not seen him since he drove us to that concert."

"We went to see The Jacksons! I remember that well. You danced so wildly you nearly poked someone's eye out! How times change," Mary said, wistfully.

As they waited, a man sitting on a bench tossed a free newspaper onto the seat beside him. Mary glanced over twice before mustering the courage to walk over. "Excuse me, are you finished with this paper?"

The man nodded curtly and turned his gaze away from her to peer into the gloom of the tunnel. Mary picked up the paper and walked back to Annabelle.

"I had forgotten how rude Londoners can be," Mary said in a whisper.

Annabelle shrugged sympathetically as her hair whirled around her face. A rumble got louder and finally, an extra-powerful gust of wind ushered the train from the tunnel into the light of the platform. Sliding doors opened and as they were reminded to "Mind the gap," the two women stepped into a carriage and sat down again. As the train started and they swayed with its motion, Mary opened the paper and perused it solemnly. She scanned the headlines, turning the pages only after she had cast her eyes across each one. Annabelle glanced curiously at her friend.

"Are you always so interested in the news, Mary?" she asked.

Mary shook her head. "No. I'm just wondering if there's something here that could be connected to the woman who handed me the note."

Annabelle tilted her head, bemused. "Such as?"

"Well, look here. A serial killer has been roaming the streets of Lewisham."

"That's nowhere near the café. And look here," Annabelle said, pointing to the top of the article, "it says they caught him."

Mary turned the page, disappointed by her poor sleuthing skills, but determined to prove her point. "What about this! Russian spy poisoned in Notting Hill. She could have easily been poisoned!"

Annabelle leant over Mary's shoulder, scanned a few paragraphs, and relaxed her brow. "It says the actual poisoning happened last year."

Mary turned the page again, deflated. Annabelle checked her watch whilst Mary continued to study the newspaper for clues. "Shall I read your horoscope, Annabelle?"

"Mary! You're a Catholic nun! You shouldn't be indulging in such poppycock!"

"Oh, it's just a bit of fun to pass the time."

"It's nonsense, and dangerous if you take it too seriously."

"Don't be such a spoilsport!"

"I'm not!" Annabelle cried. "Look at us. We have the same star sign, and yet we're entirely different."

Mary smiled mischievously. "And we're also very alike, wouldn't you say?"

Annabelle rolled her eyes in defeat. "Okay, go on then."

Mary folded up the paper eagerly, exposing only the quarter page that listed the daily astrological pronouncements. She opened her mouth to recite the words, then lowered her eyebrows, shocked and confused.

Annabelle leant forwards, waiting for her to speak. "Well?"

Mary shifted in her seat, and cleared her throat, before speaking in a slow, serious tone. "'Today will be a day of dramatic events. Stay alert, because someone you know will be full of surprises.'"

The two women looked at each other for a few seconds. Annabelle broke the silence with a snort of derision. "Nonsense. That's so general, it could apply to almost anyone, or anything, on any day. Here's our stop. Let's go."

As they hurried through the station, the shock of the day's horoscope seemed to spur just a little more speed from the pair. They left Baker Street station like a couple of scampering dogs, and after stopping briefly to ask for directions to Glentworth Street, maintained a brisk pace all the way to the entrance of the enormous property whose address they had been given over the phone.

CHAPTER SIX

ANNABELLE PRESSED THE bell eagerly. When the door buzzed without a word from the intercom, she grabbed the door handle and pushed forcefully. Mary followed her inside, somehow keeping up with Annabelle's long strides as they climbed up the stairs to the flat. By the time they stood on the threshold, they were panting from the climb and the excitement, but keen to finally meet the mysterious Teresa.

Mary raised her hand ready to knock, but before she did so the door slowly opened to reveal a short woman who was no doubt the Teresa they had come to see. She was well-dressed in khaki slacks and an intricately knitted cardigan in duck egg blue. The wrinkles on her face seemed well-earned. Her deep brown eyes hinted at many adventures. Her white hair was still thick enough to frame her face elegantly, and when she spoke, her voice had the strong, aged woodiness of a classical instrument.

"Hello. I've been waiting for you. Do come in," the woman said.

"Thank you," Mary replied, stepping into the hallway. Annabelle followed, politely nodding her appreciation.

The flat was lavish, open, and large. It was filled to bursting point. There were ornate sculptures, powerfully evocative artwork, and ornaments polished to a high sheen. Mixed among them were crucifixes, elaborate carvings of the Virgin Mary, and diamond-encrusted plates that depicted scenes involving saints. There was nowhere for the eye to rest.

Annabelle and Mary stepped forwards carefully, fearful of spoiling what seemed like one of the most personal and packed museum exhibitions they had ever seen. Teresa trudged past them. She had a slight limp. The elderly woman led them through to a living room packed with just as many objects of fine craftsmanship as the entrance hall.

"Please, take a seat. I've laid out some tea," Teresa said.

Annabelle's instincts told her that there was something strange about her and the situation they were in, but when she caught sight of the table, she relaxed. Laid out was an elegant china tea service. Detailed floral patterns were printed tastefully on each piece. Annabelle's eyes immediately focused on a plate of small slices of cake. With her connoisseur's eye for sweets, she could tell they would be delicious and that whatever was causing the peculiar feelings stirring in Annabelle's chest could wait. "Oh, this looks delightful." The vicar beamed.

Teresa held Annabelle's gaze as if assessing her, a small, slightly reticent smile on her face. "Please, sit."

Once they had settled themselves, Teresa leant over the table and began pouring tea. "Please do try the cake," she said.

Annabelle and Mary each took one of the slices from the plate. Mary nibbled at hers, whilst Annabelle popped the entire slice into her mouth. They were only small she reasoned, more the size of a petit four, really.

"Mmm!" Annabelle murmured, as she savoured the creamy texture. "Absolutely magnificent! Oh, my!"

Teresa set the teapot down. "I call it 'Teresa's Surprise Cake.' It's my niece's favourite. She does so much for me, it feels good to repay the favour by baking one for her occasionally."

Annabelle was still sifting her tongue around her mouth, trying to capture every remnant of the extraordinary flavour. "Gosh! That might be one of the most scrumptious things I've ever eaten!"

Teresa raised an eyebrow as if she fully expected this reaction. Her eyes widened, and her smile became less tentative. When she spoke again, it was with a new air of confidence. "I'm so glad you like it. I have more in the kitchen. You must take some home with you."

Annabelle's eyes lit up, all thoughts of danger and death having disappeared from her mind. "That would be wonderful! Thank you ever so much!"

Teresa nodded and left the room through a doorway Annabelle assumed led to the kitchen. She was still smiling so much at the thought of enjoying the cake again (something she believed she thoroughly deserved after the morning's events), that she barely noticed Mary's persistent nudging.

"Annabelle!" Mary whispered, as aggressively as she could muster—which wasn't very aggressive at all. "You should tell her what happened! I can't! This is all too much for me."

"Yes, alright!" Annabelle said, matching Mary's hushed tones. "Don't worry."

Teresa returned clutching two clear plastic bags. Visible

inside them were the cakes wrapped in aluminium foil. "I hope you don't mind," she said. "Wrapping them up like this is all I could manage at short notice."

"Oh, of course," Annabelle said, gleefully taking the two bags and handing one to Mary. "Why do you call it 'Teresa's Surprise Cake'?"

"Because it has a very rare, very secret ingredient," Teresa said.

Annabelle's eyes lit up as brightly as fireworks. "That sounds utterly thrilling! Doesn't it, Mary?"

Mary shook her head vigorously, but her face was consumed with anxiety. Annabelle saw it, and her expression changed to one more appropriate for the subject she was about to raise. They watched as Teresa slowly moved to sit in a chair by the open window.

"I like to sit here," Teresa said as if reading their thoughts, "and keep watch. I rarely leave the flat. My niece runs most of my errands."

"Oh," Mary said, "well, it's wonderful. I would find myself quite happily occupied among so many delightful things."

"Thank you," Teresa said. "My ex-husband was one of the greatest antique dealers in the world. He dealt in only the most beautiful and rarest objects."

Annabelle was loath to interrupt Teresa's reminiscences —particularly with such dreadful news—but there was no alternative "Teresa," she began in a serious tone, "we believe you may be in grave danger. You were supposed to meet Sister Mary today to discuss funding for her African mission. Instead, a person handed her a note that said you were in danger. A-A person who then died," Annabelle added.

Teresa's smile froze on her face as pain filled her eyes. "No!" she cried. She clutched the arms of her chair and looked wildly around her. She opened her mouth and closed it again without speaking. Then, in an act of apparent defeat, Teresa slumped back in her chair as if all the life and fight had gone out of her.

Annabelle jumped up and held Teresa's hand, patting the back of it. "There, there," she cooed.

Teresa looked up at her, imploring. "I . . . know that I'm . . . in danger . . ." she said. She was slurring her words. "I . . . know . . . something . . . danger . . ." Annabelle and Mary watched her, dumbfounded at the sudden change in the elderly woman. Before either of them could offer any help, Teresa let out one last broken syllable and clattered forwards out of her chair onto the jewel-toned Persian rug in front of it.

"Teresa?" Annabelle gasped. She looked at Mary, who yet again clasped her hand over her mouth. The two of them looked at each other in shock until Mary's nursing instincts kicked in. She sprang into action.

"Teresa, are you okay?" Mary said as she kneeled beside the fallen woman. She gently pressed a hand to Teresa's shoulder. When there was no response, Mary looked at Annabelle, her eyes wide. Annabelle desperately scanned the room for some answer as to Teresa's collapse.

With the care of a well-practiced nurse, Mary lifted Teresa a little and placed two delicate fingers on her neck. She closed her eyelids momentarily as her worst fears were confirmed. "Annabelle, she's dead."

"Are you sure?"

"Yes. The way she collapsed . . . It was almost exactly like the woman at the café. I was just about to say some . . ."

Mary's expression changed as she noticed something in the crease of Teresa's neck.

"What is it?" Annabelle asked.

Mary showed Annabelle a tiny hair-like sliver of something clear and sharp, just short of two inches long.

"It's . . . cold . . . Like a shard of ice. Look, it's melting," Mary said, twisting the fragment in her fingers.

Annabelle leant over to get a closer look. "You're right," she said, before opening her eyes wide in terror. She smacked the object out of Mary's hand.

"Ow! Annabelle!" Mary screamed, clutching at her hand.

"I'm awfully sorry, Mary, but a thought just occurred to me."

"What kind of horrible thought would cause you to hit me?"

"Check Teresa's neck," Annabelle said, also kneeling beside the woman. "Where you found that shard of ice." Mary scowled at her friend before doing as she said.

"Well, the skin is rather crepey . . . But look here," she said, pointing. "There's a little redness around this tiny dot. It looks like a puncture wound."

Mary and Annabelle shared a look of horror. Annabelle got up and examined the open window next to Teresa's favoured chair.

"Come on, Mary! We have to leave immediately!" Annabelle flapped her hands, urging Mary to get up from the floor.

"But, what about . . . ?"

"We have to leave her, Mary! We must get out of here, quickly. Come on!"

Annabelle grabbed Mary's hand. They ran through the flat with none of the care they had shown upon entering until Annabelle slid to a stop. She quickly turned and ran back the way she had come.

"Where are you going, Annabelle?" Mary yelled.

"The cakes!" Annabelle cried, emerging from the living room seconds later carrying the two bags aloft. "We almost left them behind!"

CHAPTER SEVEN

AS SOON AS the two friends had scarpered from the flat and back to the populated safety of Baker Street, Annabelle found a phone box. She called the emergency services, then DI Cutcliffe.

"Meet me outside the flat in an hour," Cutcliffe told them. "We need to investigate the area."

Annabelle and Mary secreted themselves in a small café, clutching each other and casting nervous glances about them as if surrounded by wolves. When the aforementioned time was up, they locked arms and slowly made their way back to Glentworth Street, their nerves jangling until the sight of multiple police and ambulance vehicles afforded them a feeling of safety.

As they drew close, joining the dozen or so onlookers who watched the covered stretcher being wheeled into the back of an ambulance, Cutcliffe suddenly appeared before them as if rising from below ground. His pen and notepad were at the ready.

"So, ladies," he said in his gruff voice, "you should know the drill by now. From the top, if you please."

Mary looked at Annabelle in the hope she would take the lead, which she promptly did. "Mary received a note from the woman who died at the café earlier this morning," Annabelle said, pulling out the slip of paper and handing it to DI Cutcliffe. "One that said Teresa, the woman now in the ambulance there, was in danger. There was a phone number . . ."

"And you didn't think that was worth mentioning when I questioned you this morning?" Cutcliffe directed this to Mary, a sort of verbal jab.

"I completely forgot about it! It was only later when I found the note that I remembered it!" Mary pleaded. She was exasperated and overwhelmed by both her shortcomings and the situation. "Oh, Detective Inspector! Please, I know it sounds terribly negligent, but this is all happening so fast! I'm a nun. I am used to solemn worship. Slow, deliberate thought. All of this is much more confusing and stressful than anything I'm accustomed to!"

Cutcliffe's frown remained despite Mary's pleading. "But you found the note, and instead of calling me, you visited this *Teresa*."

"When the note mentioned danger," Annabelle said, stepping in to offer some clarity on behalf of her frazzled friend, "we never interpreted it to mean immediate, *fatal* danger. Surely, the woman at the café would have gone straight to the police had it been so. Instead, she handed Sister Mary, a nun, a note. We had every intention of telling you, Detective Inspector, but we had hoped to discover more about the situation before placing the task at your door."

Cutcliffe swivelled his eyes to look at Annabelle, although he remained facing Mary. It was as if he suspected them both.

"It was my idea, Detective Inspector, and I'm incredibly regretful about it now," Annabelle added.

Acknowledging Annabelle's apology, the detective offered a barely perceptible nod, before proceeding to angrily scribble in his notebook. "So you visited the flat, and then what?"

"Teresa invited us in," Mary said, eager to answer a question that didn't depict her as worthy of suspicion, "and we sat down to take tea. We told her what had happened in the morning, and then she collapsed in almost the exact same manner as the woman at the café."

DI Cutcliffe raised an eyebrow so heavy, it seemed to require a lot of effort. "You said nothing else to each other?"

"We exchanged pleasantries," Annabelle said, looking at Mary for confirmation.

"We complimented the flat," Mary added.

The detective raised his other eyebrow. "You complimented the flat?"

"Why yes," Mary said, "it's full of wonder and beauty."

Cutcliffe jabbed the end of his pen back over his shoulder. "That mess? You complimented it? You've got some weird taste in furnishings."

"Mess, Detective Inspector?" Annabelle was taken aback by DI Cutcliffe's poor taste and his crude manner of expressing himself. "How can you call a place so full of history, of beauty, of rarefied artefacts, a mess?"

"Easily," the detective responded, "when there's junk piled from floor to ceiling, and it looks like it hasn't been cleaned in a year." Annabelle and Mary gasped. "Are you saying it wasn't like that when you arrived?"

"Not at all, Detective Inspector!" Mary exclaimed. "Why, it was immaculate. We barely breathed heavily in case we blew something out of place."

Cutcliffe scribbled so much into his notebook that he had to flip a page. He did it angrily as if irritated that he needed to do so.

"Do you think someone entered the flat after us and wrecked it, Detective Inspector?" Annabelle asked.

"If you're telling the truth," DI Cutcliffe responded, the veracity of Annabelle's and Mary's characters clearly still uncertain, "then that's precisely what happened."

"Who would do such a thing?" Mary asked.

"I have some ideas," Cutcliffe said, glancing back at his officers, who were now cordoning off the area. "So this Teresa collapses. Then what?"

"I went to her, checked her pulse, and discovered that she was dead. I'm a nurse, you see," Mary added. This statement started another bout of manic note-taking. "I found something very curious, actually. A thin shard of ice embedded in her neck. I checked for a puncture wound and found one."

"Hold on," the detective said, raising his hand. "You're saying there was a piece of ice *in her neck*? Like some kind of dart?"

"That's what we believe," Annabelle answered, "yes, Detective Inspector."

"And where is this *dart* now?"

"It was melting," Mary said after a few seconds thought. "I held it, but Annabelle knocked it out of my hand when we realised it might have caused Teresa's death."

"I imagine it melted away long ago, Detective Inspector," Annabelle said.

"Convenient," came Cutcliffe's reply. He continued to write.

"Detective Inspector!" Annabelle cried. "You do not

seriously believe that we caused this horrible death, do you?"

Cutcliffe noisily flipped to a fresh page in his notebook and raised his fearsome eyes to meet Annabelle's. His eyebrows wriggled like hairy caterpillars.

"I believe nothing in my line of work. I just deal with the facts. You have been at the site of two suspicious deaths within the past three hours. The woman at the café was poisoned, and I would bet a sizeable chunk of my pension that this Teresa died in the same way." Mary gasped. The detective handed his notebook and pen to Annabelle. "This time I want *your* contact details and phone number," he said firmly.

Annabelle huffed but took the pen and the notebook from Cutcliffe. "The idea we had anything to do with this is laughable!"

"Really? You're telling me that an *ice dart* that has *melted away* has killed one, probably two of your associates in the space of a few hours. You're telling me that a flat that looks like wild elephants have run through it was immaculate and worthy of compliments just an hour ago. Likely stories—not impossible, but not probable either."

Annabelle handed back the pen and notepad. "But . . ."

"The most infuriating thing," Cutcliffe interrupted, "is that you withheld evidence. Not only did you hold back a critical piece of information, but you acted upon it yourselves."

"It was . . ." Mary started.

The detective raised his square hand to silence her. "And to top it off, after witnessing the death of a defenceless old woman, you're off buying cakes! What are they?" Cutcliffe said, grasping Annabelle's wrist and lifting it to glare at the bags she still clutched in her hand. The triangular slices wrapped in foil were clearly visible inside. "Chocolate?"

"We didn't . . ."

"I've heard enough. When I need to speak to you—and I certainly will need to speak more to both of you—I'll be in touch. Until then, stay where I can reach you."

"But I can't!" Mary cried. "I have to return to Africa!"

The detective shook his owl-like head. "That will not happen. Like it or not, you are embroiled in a double-murder case. You'll stay where I can get hold of you and feel lucky I haven't thrown you into a cell. Yet."

Annabelle opened her mouth to reply. But by the time she had thought of something to say, the detective was striding away from them back to the flat, shouting orders at his constables.

Annabelle and Mary sat beside each other in silence on the way home. If the earlier part of the day had brought to mind fond memories of their schoolgirl adventures, their second meeting with DI Cutcliffe had reminded them of the inevitable scoldings when things went too far. They stared into space.

"What are you thinking?" Annabelle said after almost ten minutes of quiet contemplation. It was the same phrase she had used as a girl when breaking a lengthy silence between them.

"I'm thinking about how to explain all this to Mother Superior. I'm thinking about all the people I'll have to inform about my delayed return to Africa and how disappointed they'll be when I tell them I didn't get the funding." Mary said this as slowly and as carefully as she said her prayers. Annabelle cast a determined look at her bag of cake, her eyes narrowing.

"What are you thinking?" Mary asked.

"I'm thinking about how we're going to solve this case," Annabelle replied.

Mary stiffened and turned to Annabelle, all steadiness disappearing from her voice. "Solve the case? We can't solve the case!" she screeched.

"Why ever not?" Annabelle said. "We are two smart, confident women of God."

"But we're already under suspicion!"

"All the more reason we need to fix this terrible situation! The inspector obviously didn't believe us about the ice dart and the tidy flat but we know it's true. And that means we're in a much better position to uncover the actual murderer than the inspector is. And if we do nothing, we may find ourselves put on the block for lack of better suspects!"

"Oh, Annabelle," Mary said, slumping back into her seat, "you will get us into an even bigger mess!"

"No, I won't. Let's meet for lunch tomorrow and make plans."

"Alright," Mary said wearily. "This is your stop."

"Oh yes," Annabelle said. "See you tomorrow. Say hello to Mother Superior for me when you speak to her."

Before Annabelle got off the train, she handed Mary her cake and pocketed hers. She made her way back to St. Clement's church, her thoughts still with her friend, who would have a lot of explaining to do when she returned to the rectory where she was staying.

A few minutes later, when Annabelle walked into her imposing church, she heard the clink of teacups coming from the kitchen at the back. She walked in to find Cecilia

Robinson, church secretary, cleaner, and expert tea-maker pottering about.

"Hello, Reverend," she said in her cheery Manchester accent. "You must have had a busy day. I've not seen you at all. Tea?"

"The words 'yes' and 'please' have never felt so insufficient," Annabelle said. "Oh," she squealed suddenly, fishing around in her sizeable cassock pocket. "I've got cake."

"Don't bother," Cecilia said, "Mrs. O'Dwyer brought in some of your favourite cherry cupcakes this afternoon. You know what they're like; soft as snow when she's just made them, hard as rock the morning after." Annabelle caught sight of the pile of cherry-dotted crumbling magnificence Cecilia had placed on the table and completely forgot about Teresa's cake.

"Just when I was beginning to question my faith," Annabelle said.

Cecilia tutted. Despite her dark past, Cecilia had rebuilt her life around the Lord, and she was now in possession of faith so deep it would take a shovel to shake it. She put a lot of priests to shame.

Annabelle took the mug of milky tea that Cecilia offered her and picked out what she deemed the largest cupcake.

"Father John is here, Reverend."

Annabelle raised her eyebrows and gave Cecilia a quizzical look, her mouth fully occupied with cake.

"Apparently, a Catholic bishop has called twice today, asking about you," Cecilia explained. "I spoke to Father John when he arrived. He said he'd wait an hour before calling the bishop back. He's in the vestry."

Annabelle chewed slowly, swallowed, and pursed her lips.

"Is something wrong, Reverend?"

"Yes," replied Annabelle.

"What is it?"

Annabelle held the cupcake aloft to inspect it in the light. "Mrs. O'Dwyer has used tinned cherries."

CHAPTER EIGHT

THE OFFICE OF St. Clement's church was Annabelle's pride and joy. Originally, it had begun life as a room for the presiding priest to change into clerical garments, gain some respite, and to store things. Over the years, however, many incumbents had added to and refined the room's purpose. Its size and the large window that overlooked the giant sycamore trees in the church grounds made it an enticing place to spend time. A bookcase added here, an oak desk there, some leather seats, an expertly carved prayer stand, and the room was now a fully-fledged office from which Annabelle could conduct all manner of affairs.

As Annabelle stepped inside the warm and inviting room, Father John pulled himself away from his Bible and leapt up out of an office chair. "Annabelle! Where on earth have you been?" he exclaimed, as she dropped onto the couch next to the desk.

"Oh, Father," Annabelle replied, still new enough in her position that she referred to him by his title. "I have just experienced one of the most eventful days I believe I've ever had."

"I've been trying to reach you for hours. I do wish you would take your phone with you when you go out."

"I assure you, Father, I only intended to be away for an hour or two. I left my phone here as I hate interruptions. Mobile phones are terribly rude."

"Well, this is exactly the sort of circumstance in which they're also *terribly* useful." Father John began pace the floor in front of Annabelle. "Bishop Murphy—he of the Catholic Church, no less—has called multiple times. He left a message."

"What did he say?"

Father John shrugged. "He'd like to speak to you. He was insistent. I believe it has something to do with whatever bother you managed to get into today. You were with Sister . . ."

"Mary."

"Yes, Mary. He'll likely want to speak to her, too."

Annabelle sighed. Father John pitched up his trouser legs as he leant back against the desk, folded his arms, and looked at Annabelle with the patience of a sympathetic parent. "What happened today? Tell me everything."

Annabelle shook her head and took a deep breath. She figured out where to start, and began. The meeting with Mary, the identical deaths, DI Cutcliffe's penetrating questions, and Mary's struggles to explain herself, all tumbled out. When Annabelle had described every event in detail, she looked at Father John's confused face, and asked, "What should I do?"

Father John scratched at his short, well-pruned beard as he considered the question. "That's an astonishing story," he said. "To witness not just one death but two? In the space of a few hours. It's incredible. You can hardly blame DI Cutcliffe for being suspicious." Annabelle smacked her thighs in disappointment at his dispiriting but fair appraisal.

The senior cleric continued. "But I know DI Cutcliffe well. He's a talented detective. He wouldn't have allowed you to leave if he suspected you as much as you think he does, though it's possible he may be giving you just enough rope with which to hang yourself."

"Would he really do that?"

"As I said, he's a talented detective, he works somewhat unconventionally."

Father John cast a look at Annabelle that made her jaw clench. "What is it?" she said, curious to discover whatever thoughts had caused him to look at her like that. "What are you thinking?"

Father John raised his hand. "Now, don't be offended, this is just an idea I find myself unable to shake. It's the most obvious question that springs to mind." Annabelle squinted as she tried to work out where the senior priest was leading her.

"This Sister Mary," he said, slowly, "how well do you actually know her?"

"Just what are you insinuating?" Annabelle gasped, her hands shooting to her hips. "Mary and I have been friends since we were babies! Why, she was born in the back of the very taxi my father drove!"

"Yes, yes," Father John acknowledged. "You've told me that before. But you haven't seen her in a while, correct?"

"Two years, but if there's one person in this world I would trust, it's Mary. She's one of the kindest, gentlest, most beautiful human beings I've ever had the wonderful fortune to meet!"

Father John nodded. He stood and paced a little. "I'm

sure of it. You're an excellent judge of character, Annabelle. It's just . . ."

Annabelle watched him walk up and down, her head following his path as if she were observing a very slow tennis match.

"Well," he continued, "the whole encounter seems very strange. Are you sure your friend is sensible? Seems a little odd to arrange a meeting with a woman about whom she had virtually no knowledge."

"Mary's been very busy since she arrived in London." Annabelle spoke firmly as if objecting in a court of law.

"But she *forgot* to give Cutcliffe the slip of paper, only showing it to you later. And from what you've told me, it was she who discovered the ice dart in the victim's neck. She might have put it there."

"Nonsense! She was trying to help!"

"Was there a moment when you couldn't see this Teresa and Sister Mary at the same time? A split-second, even?" Annabelle opened her mouth to refute his suggestion before closing it again.

"What is it?" urged Father John.

"Well, there was one moment. Teresa offered us cake, and I spent a few moments . . ."

Father John waited before saying: "Yes?"

". . . My eyes were closed—I was enjoying my cake. But that doesn't mean anything! Mary's involvement in these deaths is an entirely ludicrous idea, Father and I'm gravely disappointed in you for even thinking there might be some substance to it!"

"I'm just considering the possibilities, Annabelle," Father John said, in a kindly voice. "I assure you, DI Cutcliffe won't be nearly as merciless once he's conducted his preliminary investigations."

"I suppose," Annabelle said.

"Look, here we have a nurse who is no doubt well-acquainted with concoctions that can kill as well as heal, who has recently returned from Africa where poisons are still used, and who was close to two suspicious deaths that occurred within hours of one another. It's all rather incriminating."

"That's what the detective said. But why, Father? Why would Mary do anything like this?"

"You said yourself that she needed funding. Perhaps the murders were tied to that somehow—or perhaps the entire idea of funding her hospital in Africa is a front for something else."

Annabelle stood up angrily, her hands finding her hips again. "I would sooner send myself to the gallows than believe Mary is guilty of such things! She's innocent in every sense of the word! All you've done, Father, is further convince me that it is imperative that I find the truth behind what went on today and do so quickly!"

Father John looked at Annabelle and smiled, impressed. "Your faith in your friend appears steadfast. You're extremely noble, Annabelle, but it's always worth remembering that blind faith can lead us astray as easily as it can fortify us."

"This is not about faith, Father. I know her to be innocent. I know Mary."

"Very well. Then you should consider other possibilities."

"What are they?" Annabelle asked, settling down again onto the couch.

"In my experience, such closely timed, similar deaths are usually gang-related. Or, at the very least, some kind of family feud. This situation seems coordinated enough for that, but an old lady . . . hmm, that is unusual. Look, we could spend all night making up conspiracy theories. What you need right now is a good night's rest. We can talk about this again tomorrow.

"In the meantime, the one thing you must do, Annabelle, is co-operate with the police. Trust DI Cutcliffe to do his job. He rarely gets it wrong, and if, rather like your cake, there are further layers to this, he will uncover them. You could even bring up the matter of your faith in Sister Mary when you speak to Bishop Murphy. He's a smart man, and if things do get a little . . . heated for your friend—or yourself—then you'll need his help."

"Thank you, Father." Annabelle sighed, soothed by his confidence and authority. "I don't know what I would do without you."

Father John smiled at her and shook his head. "And I don't know what I'm going to do *with* you."

CHAPTER NINE

S INCE MOVING TO London, Annabelle had ensured that until she had eaten breakfast, she would not let the day's responsibilities rush into her mind. Instead, she would use the serenity of her early morning routine to contemplate her privileged position, refine her sense of faith, and reflect upon her personal growth.

However, on the morning after the terrible events surrounding Mary, Teresa, and the young woman at the café, Annabelle made an exception. She brushed her teeth purposefully, dressed in expectation of all surprises, and ate a hearty breakfast that she hoped would give her the fortitude to handle the day's investigation.

Her first task was to call Bishop Murphy. She gathered her composure, braced herself for addressing such an important figure, albeit from a different branch of the church, and made the call. Rather anticlimactically, the bishop was not available, but his secretary assured Annabelle that she was welcome to call back later.

With some time left before her lunch meeting with

Mary and after a brief, pleasant conversation with Cecilia, Annabelle set off on a walk. Minding Father John's words of the previous day, she remembered to take her mobile phone with her. As she slipped it into her pocket, she found the bag of cake still there. "Hmm, might need that later," she murmured, patting her pocket. "For energy. There's a long day ahead."

As she walked, Annabelle mulled over the prior day's events before calling Mary to confirm their meeting. Mary sounded even more stressed after a night of sleep, and they agreed to meet in Soho, a densely packed district in the very heart of London. It was busy throughout the day, which meant it should be safe and was far from the sites of the two murders. There was also a rather enticingly colourful tea shop about which Annabelle had heard positive things.

After her walk through the streets and parks of London, Annabelle braved the bus again. She caught the number twenty-nine to Leicester Square. She would walk to Soho from there. As Annabelle stepped off the bus, the sun warmed her face and she witnessed the pleasing scene of a crowded London street at midday. Tourists, shoppers, workers, and hordes of foreign students milled around her. It was difficult to feel the proximity of evil in such surroundings, however much Annabelle reminded herself to stay alert to danger. She strolled along the pavement with a smile, enjoying the reactions of Londoners for whom a smiling pedestrian was as alarming as a crazy one, and after ten minutes she reached the tea shop feeling full of affection for her fellow man.

The bell above the door tinkled as Annabelle entered the tea shop, she nodded a cheerful hello to the proprietor behind the counter. After scanning the tables, she noticed Mary, her hand politely raised to gain Annabelle's attention.

Mary sat at the back of the room clutching an orange cup. Today, she wore her habit. On the table next to her was a small, discreet brown leather purse. Annabelle bought herself a cup of tea and a chocolate caramel bar and carried them to the table.

"Mary! How are you?" Annabelle said after they exchanged a quick embrace and settled into comfortably old-fashioned chairs.

"I feel awful, Annabelle," Mary muttered.

"Did you tell everyone what happened?"

"I told them I had to stay in London a little longer than I had intended, but I didn't say precisely why. Oh Annabelle, I couldn't! I was far too frightened of what they might think of me."

"I'm sure it'll turn out fine."

Mary shook her head. "So much depends on me, Annabelle. In Africa, people are dying daily from easily curable diseases and other afflictions. We work almost around the clock with minimal resources. We put every penny we have towards drugs and treatments that help people survive. Even small donations help, but there are so many people in need that we require a lot of money. That was my task. That's why I'm here, to get funding. And instead, I'll return penniless!"

Mary seemed on the verge of tears. Annabelle placed a hand over her friend's and rubbed it supportively.

"Don't worry, Mary. We'll get to the bottom of this. I promise."

Mary looked into Annabelle's eyes. "Oh Annabelle, you don't still want to . . . *investigate* this, do you? We're in enough trouble as it is."

"Well, actually, I think I might be on to something," Annabelle said, leaning forwards to gain her friend's full attention. "Do you recall what Detective Inspector Cutcliffe said about Teresa's flat? Shortly after we had left it?"

Mary thought for a few seconds, before latching on to what Annabelle was referring to. "About it being in complete disarray?"

"Yes!" Annabelle exclaimed.

"It was rather strange . . ." Mary agreed.

"There must have been someone else who entered the house after us, who then ransacked the flat."

"The person who killed her, perhaps?" Mary said. Her eyes shone, Annabelle's enthusiasm was catching.

"Very possibly. Likely, I would say. They must have killed Teresa so they could enter her flat with no one seeing."

"But why? I don't understand why someone would destroy such a beautiful home."

Annabelle wagged a finger and smiled sneakily. "What if they were looking for something?"

Mary placed her palms on the table and glanced around. "One of her artefacts, perhaps! There must have been some priceless valuables among all those pieces," she whispered.

"Precisely," Annabelle hissed, pleased to find her friend joining in with her deductions.

"But why kill her whilst we were there? Wouldn't it have been much easier to do it beforehand or wait until we had left? Then the thief could have easily taken what he—or she—wanted from the flat, and no one would have been any the wiser. Did they not know we were there? Could that have been merely an extraordinary coincidence?"

Annabelle nodded, then took a sip of her tea. When she

looked back into Mary's face, there were deep frown lines between her eyes.

"I believe that wasn't a coincidence," Annabelle said deliberately. "I don't see how they couldn't have known we were there. We were clearly visible through the windows."

"Then why not wait until we had left?"

"Mary," Annabelle said, using the tone of her voice to prepare her friend for a statement she wished she didn't believe as much as she did, "I believe someone is trying to frame us. More accurately, I believe they're trying to frame *you*."

CHAPTER TEN

MARY'S HAND WASN'T quick enough to smother the loud shriek she emitted. Tea drinkers sitting at the surrounding tables whipped their heads around to see where the high-pitched scream came from. Annabelle sat up in her seat and beamed. "It's alright," she assured them, "she's never tasted a chocolate caramel bar before."

As the tea shop patrons returned to their conversations, Annabelle turned back to Mary who had now calmed herself enough such that she was able to speak. "Frame me? Why would anyone seek to frame *me* of all people?" Mary said.

"That's one of the questions that's been troubling me since I woke up," Annabelle replied.

"And who would do such a thing, anyway?"

"That's the other question," Annabelle said, taking a sizeable bite from her caramel bar.

They sat silently, sipping their tea and considering the questions that hung in the air between them. Every once in a while, Mary would frown and sigh sadly. Annabelle could feel the strain that her friend was under as keenly as if it were her own.

"Oh Annabelle," Mary said, eventually, "where will this all end? I don't see how I'll ever get out of this pickle. At best, I'll return to Africa late, disgraced, and without any of the money I tried so hard to get. At worst . . . I daren't think about it, but if I am being framed, then I won't just be punished, I'll bring huge amounts of shame to the work my fellow nuns are doing all over Africa, perhaps the entire Catholic Church!"

"I'm sure it won't be as bad as that."

"I can't share your optimism, Annabelle. Can you imagine what the papers would say if they found out? A nun? Accused of murder—and possibly stealing? It would make the front pages! The indignity!"

Annabelle sipped her tea. She wished she could calm her friend's worries, but to deny them would be a lie. Mary was right. If the newspapers did find out, the ensuing mess would be dreadful for everyone involved.

"What should we do now?" Mary said, eventually. Annabelle placed her tea cup down gently. She, too, had been considering the same question.

"There's one person who can help us."

"Who?" Mary quickly said, eager to follow any avenue that might help her out of her sticky situation.

"Bishop Murphy. Apparently, he has already heard about this spot of trouble we find ourselves in. He called me multiple times yesterday and is keen to speak to me. I would imagine he'd like to speak to you too."

"He called me, but I had hoped to delay speaking to him until . . . well, until I had rather more positive news."

"Perhaps Bishop Murphy can provide us with that positive news," Annabelle said, pulling her mobile phone from her pocket.

"I should mention something before you call," Mary said, placing a hand over Annabelle's phone.

"Yes?" Annabelle said, raising an eyebrow.

Mary squirmed a little before speaking. "The bishop may not be as sympathetic towards me as you might expect. You see . . ."

Annabelle's ears pricked up. Her eyebrows followed suit. "What is it, Mary?"

"He and Teresa knew each other. I'm not sure but I believe they were friends. She was a well-known supporter of the Catholic Church. It was the bishop who suggested I seek her out. He said she might be able to help with the funding for my hospital. He is probably gravely upset about her death, not least because of my involvement—or I should say—suspected involvement."

Annabelle considered her friend's words. She pushed away the unthinkable thought that popped into her mind and smiled good-naturedly as she sought the bishop's number on her phone. "All the more reason to get him on our side as quickly as possible," she declared, bringing the phone to her ear. "Let's just hope that his judgement is as sound as his faith."

Bishop Murphy's home was in the heart of Kensington, one of London's oldest and wealthiest boroughs. With its clean, tree-lined streets and well-maintained homes, many of them vast, it was an area that attracted the kind of people who enjoyed the distinctive hustle and bustle of London life whilst still desiring peaceful, quiet streets and luxurious homes more often found in suburbia.

Annabelle and Mary felt relaxed as they strolled through the spotless streets. They walked arm in arm, just as they had when they were children in search of their next adventure.

"This is it," Annabelle said as they stopped outside the address given to her by the bishop's secretary. The bishop was eager to speak to them, the woman had told her when Annabelle had called. They could drop round anytime.

"Oh my!" Mary cried as she craned her neck to take in the full majesty of the bishop's home.

They were standing in front of a tall, four-storey Victorian building. The mansion boasted enormous arched windows, and the double front doors were almost as large as those of Annabelle's church. The white-stone walls were brighter than any other on the street, and the colourful flowers that lined the gravel path up to the door were as inviting to newcomers as they were to the bees and butterflies that frolicked among them.

"Have you ever been here before, Annabelle?"

"No. I'm incredibly curious to see what it's like inside. If it's half as striking as it is outside, we're in for a treat."

"You go first, Annabelle," Mary said as if daring her friend.

"Okay, off I go!" Annabelle chuckled breezily. She opened the gate and led the way up the path to the large steps in front of the house and the big, brass knocker that hung on the door.

CHAPTER ELEVEN

ECONDS AFTER ANNABELLE had confidently knocked on the door, a young woman dressed in a grey pencil skirt and white blouse opened it. With her black, perfectly coiffed hair, her dark brown eyes, and olive skin, Annabelle assumed the woman must be of Spanish or Italian descent. The woman smiled, revealing a set of perfect teeth, as white and as striking as the front of the building.

"You must be Sister Mary and Reverend Annabelle," she said in a husky voice. She had an accent that Annabelle couldn't quite place. "Please come in."

"Thank you," the two women responded, stepping carefully inside.

Suddenly, they felt as if they had stepped into some kind of portal, for the enormous entrance hall was more like that of a castle or a stately home than a house tucked into a corner of Kensington. To one side, there was a small, tidy desk and to the other, patterned carpeted stairs led to another floor. Like unimpressed audiences, busts on plinths guarded rooms, rooms that lay behind three closed doors. A thick, red carpet sat in the middle of the marble floor.

"Golly!" cried Annabelle, as she stepped onto the soft carpet and twisted to see the religious artwork hung high on the walls. "It looks larger inside than it does on the outside!"

"How impressive!" Mary added.

The bishop's secretary kept smiling and clasped her hands in front of her. "This property has been owned by the Catholic Church since shortly after it was built in 1822. It has been used for a multitude of purposes over the years, mostly involving visits from various Catholic officials abroad. Pope John Paul II was rather fond of stopping here when he travelled to London. Currently, as you know, it is being used by Bishop Murphy as both his principal place of residence and as his office from which he conducts his London affairs."

"It's almost inconceivable that such a place would lie behind what seems a simple, if elegant, large Kensington home," Mary said.

"It's interesting you should say that," the woman replied. "The building once had a far more elaborate—and rather striking—exterior. However, two years ago, Kensington council introduced a set of initiatives to harmonise the neighbourhood's appearance. Although various laws on matters of religious and historical importance protected the building, Bishop Murphy agreed to have the façade modified, so it was more in line with the area's aesthetics."

"There are twelve rooms in the building, eight bathrooms and a kitchen. There's also a temperature-controlled cellar in which items of value or religious significance are stored and occasionally displayed to select visitors."

"How interesting!" Annabelle cried.

"My name is Sara," the woman said, holding out her

hand. "I'm Bishop Murphy's secretary. He's expecting you. If you'll just hold on a second, I'll let him know you've arrived."

One afternoon, when they were children, Mary and Annabelle were called to the headmaster's office. As they had taken the solemn walk to his private rooms, they realised that the call could only mean one of two things. One, they were to receive a commendation for the recent bottle rocket project they had conducted in science class. Or two, they were about to be punished for the bottle rocket's destruction of the science classroom's ceiling, and the clothes of everyone in the room at the time. As they waited for Bishop Murphy, they shared the same mixture of foreboding and excitement they had felt that afternoon.

Sara sashayed over to the desk in a graceful manner, the like of which Annabelle could only dream of. The bishop's secretary leant over, pushed a button on a panel, and spoke briefly to her boss.

"He'll be down immediately," Sara said, flashing her fashion magazine smile at the visitors again.

"Thank you," Mary said.

Bishop Murphy was renowned for his pleasant, approachable personality, but Annabelle and Mary felt as if they were preparing for an occasion that merited all the pomp of a visit from the Queen. They stood stiffly in the entrance hall, waiting. Mary brushed a little dirt from her friend's cassock. Annabelle nodded a curt "thank you."

Soon, Bishop Murphy came down the stairs. The sense of being in the midst of a special event only increased as they watched his polished, elegant shoes emerge first, then his tailored suit, his tall, athletic build, and finally his dashing, combed-back hair.

He was well into his sixties, but Bishop Murphy had all

the vigour and presence of a man half his age. Were he not an eminent member of the Catholic Church, many would have described him as having a "roguish charm." Instead, they referred to his "energetic dynamism" and "sparkling wit."

"Hello," he said in an Irish brogue as warm and as satisfying as an excellent malt whiskey. He walked smartly over to the visitors, his hand outstretched.

"Hello, your Excellency," Mary said, shyly, wondering how such terrible events as those that had recently befallen them could result in something as prestigious as a meeting with a bishop.

"Good to see you, Sister Mary," he replied. "And you, Reverend. It's always nice to meet someone from a different branch of the church—especially someone as respected as you."

"Oh." Annabelle blushed, shaking her head at the compliment.

"Really," insisted the bishop. "I've heard a lot about the wonderful work you've done already in East London. And still so young! You've got a lot of promise, Reverend."

Annabelle sought and failed to find the appropriate words to respond to the bishop's compliment. Instead, she looked at her feet bashfully and mumbled a mild "thank you."

"Shall we go to my office?" the bishop said, turning smartly on the balls of his feet, much like a ballroom dancer. Annabelle and Mary followed him and walked through a door that the bishop held open for them.

If the entrance hall had felt like that of a palace with its marble floors, plinths, and red carpet, then the bishop's office felt like that of a grand library. Everything inside seemed carved from the richest of woods, from the book-

DEATH AT THE CAFÉ   67

shelves that covered almost every wall, to the heavy desk and green leather seats.

"You must be tired," he said, nodding at two chairs. "Take a seat. We can have a little chat."

Mary and Annabelle sat down on the ornate mahogany chairs. The bishop took a seat in a modern, well-padded leather executive chair.

"Sorry, I completely forgot—I'm so eager to talk to you! Would you like something to drink? Water? Tea? Juice?"

"No, thank you," Mary replied.

"Water would be lovely," Annabelle said.

Bishop Murphy nodded, held down a button on his intercom, and uttered a brief but polite request of Sara. Then he sat back, touched the pads of his fingers together, and smiled sympathetically.

"So . . . it seems like both of you have had some adventures this past day or two."

"Indeed," Annabelle said. She glanced at Mary. It ought to have been her who spoke to the bishop—Mary being a nun and all—but Annabelle knew her friend was feeling nervous. She decided to take the lead until Mary was comfortable enough to talk.

"So what's been going on?" the bishop inquired.

CHAPTER TWELVE

THERE WAS A knock at the office door. Sara entered carrying two bottles of water and two glasses. She laid them out in front of Annabelle and Bishop Murphy, then left quickly. After taking a sip, Annabelle began a detailed summary of the events which had occurred the previous day.

She refrained from adding any conjecture regarding the two deaths, nor did she express any of Mary's concerns, preferring to wait until the bishop offered his own views on the matters. When she finished, Annabelle took another sip of water.

"Hmm, that's quite a dramatic turn of events," Bishop Murphy said, scratching his head. He looked at the two women. "What do you make of it all?"

"I have some ideas," Annabelle said, "but I was rather hoping to hear yours."

"Well," the bishop began, "I wanted to see both of you for two reasons." Annabelle and Mary leant forwards slightly. "First, I'd like to apologise."

"Whatever for?" Mary exclaimed, bursting into life.

"I feel responsible for the situation you find yourselves in," the bishop replied. He looked at Annabelle. "I'm not sure if Sister Mary told you, Reverend, but I was the one who put her in touch with Teresa Nortega."

"Yes," Annabelle replied, "I was aware."

"I knew Teresa personally, you see. She was a wonderful member of the church. She was also fabulously wealthy, as you saw for yourselves. Her ex-husband dealt in some of the rarest artefacts and relics the world has ever seen. As she had made generous donations to the church in the past, and being particularly fond of nuns—Teresa persistently tried to get her niece, the young woman who died at the café, to join the sisterhood—I thought it would be a simple matter for Mary to approach Teresa with her funding needs."

"It was a wonderful idea, Bishop, and I'm so grateful for your help in making the introduction despite . . . despite what happened . . ." Mary trailed off.

"Don't thank me, please. I misjudged the situation entirely. I should have known something like this would happen."

"How?" exclaimed Mary, almost leaping out of her seat. "How were you to know that someone would kill Ms. Nortega? Why would anyone do such a thing?"

Bishop Murphy paused for a long moment, staring intently at Mary. "That's the second reason I brought you here," he said, slowly. "I think I may know the 'why', but I'm still trying to figure out the 'who'."

Annabelle gasped. Mary's hand flew to her mouth. Slowly, the bishop filled his glass with water, picked it up, and placed it on the other side of the desk, in front of Mary. As if in a trance, she took it and sipped. The air felt thick with anticipation and when the bishop spoke again, his sonorous voice reverberated around the room, sending chills down the spines of the two women.

"Teresa recently took ownership of something extremely valuable, a collection of items sought after by every collector and appreciator of fine things the world over."

Annabelle and Mary leant forwards further, their mouths open, just as they had as young children when an adult read them a captivating story for the first time.

"What?" Mary breathed. "What did she own that was so valuable?"

The bishop eyed Mary so keenly, that Annabelle suspected he was trying to read her thoughts. "The 'Cats-Eye' emeralds."

In the pause that followed, Annabelle and Mary glanced at each other. There was no need for speech. They could read each other's thoughts intuitively.

"They are known so," the bishop continued, "because they are jewels of such high purity, and cut with such precision, that when it is dark, they sparkle even more brightly—such is their ability to catch even the dimmest of light. Their history is shrouded in mystery. There are stories that they were cut by one of the greatest lapidarists of the sixteenth century, but no one is sure. In fact, for the past century or so, no one has had any idea where these emeralds were, or if they even existed. Until last week.

"Teresa's ex-husband held an exhibition of his rarest *objets d'art* here, in London, just six days ago. Among the items were the emeralds. Even though it was a private exhibition, inevitably, word got out. There's not a collector worth his salt who hasn't been voraciously inquiring about the emeralds ever since. Eventually, it became known that they had been gifted to Teresa and that she could do with them as she wished. No one knows why."

"But," Mary said, "no matter how valuable and lovely they are, they're not worth the lives of two women!"

Bishop Murphy leant back in his chair, a disappointed look crossing his face. "Of course, that is true," he said, "to you and I, but don't underestimate the desire attached to these jewels by some. Every day, people commit great sins for the possession of wealth, and the Cats-Eye emeralds are something almost entirely beyond that. They are the definition of priceless."

"So you think someone committed a double murder so they could steal the emeralds?" Annabelle asked.

"I don't think it," the bishop said, "I know it." He again looked at them both, one after the other. "I spoke with DI Cutcliffe as soon as I heard of Teresa's death. I informed him of the situation regarding the emeralds, after which he searched her flat. They were gone."

"Oh, dear!" Mary cried, breaking the tension with a high-pitched squeal. "This is terrible!"

"Shush, Mary, it will be alright," Annabelle said, leaning out of her seat to put a comforting hand on Mary's knee. "Bishop Murphy, this is truly a terrible situation, and we want to help however we can." The bishop raised his thick eyebrows. "But Mary was to return to Africa in a few days along with the funding she had hoped to raise. This awful mess has scuppered all her plans. Detective Inspector Cutcliffe demands that she stay. He possibly even suspects her, as ridiculous as that idea is."

"I'm not surprised," Bishop Murphy mused.

"Surely you can help her, if not with the investigation, then at least within the church." Annabelle looked to her friend, who was staring into her lap, trying her hardest to suppress sobs. "She's concerned that her reputation will be in tatters, not least because she'll return without the funding she came for."

"Yes, I see," the bishop said, deep in thought.

"And . . . well . . . " Annabelle stammered, finding it difficult to express out loud what she was thinking. "Well, you were the one who gave her Teresa's number . . ."

"Meaning it was my fault?" Bishop Murphy said with wry humour.

"Gosh, no!" Annabelle protested. "I simply meant that you know more than anyone how unlikely it is that Mary killed two women . . ." There came another brief squeal from Mary which she stifled with a handkerchief. ". . . Or stole the emeralds. Perhaps you could put in a good word for her with the police?"

Mary shot Annabelle a surprised glance. "Oh, I . . ."

"I mean, if it's not terribly bothersome for you. I understand this is a big request and . . . and . . ." Annabelle stammered.

Bishop Murphy chuckled and raised his hand for Annabelle to stop speaking. "Yes, of course. I'll make some calls and ensure you get back to Africa in time, Mary. I will make no mention of this unfortunate affair. There is no need to worry on that score, the Catholic Church will take care of you."

CHAPTER THIRTEEN

"REALLY?" MARY EXCLAIMED, her eyes as big and brilliant as a child's on Fireworks Night.

"You're a nun in the Catholic Church. No one will seriously believe that you are a double murderess, but the police have to do their job. I'm just sorry that this has wrecked your trip and your plans for funding, but I'll make some calls regarding that at the first opportunity. Perhaps we can rescue the situation."

"Oh, Your Excellency! That's so . . . benevolent of you! I'm . . . speechless!" Mary said, bowing her head. "I wish there was some way in which I could repay you."

Annabelle smiled warmly. The frown lines and dull eyes that plagued Mary had disappeared.

The bishop brushed Mary's response aside, however. "You repay the Catholic Church greatly with the work you do in Africa. It's something of which we are all immensely proud."

Mary smiled, her hands in her lap, her knees jogging

with excitement. "I feel as if the world's weight has been lifted from my shoulders!" she said to Annabelle.

Annabelle beamed Mary's smile back at her as perfectly as a reflection, but then she said, thoughtfully, "I do wonder who stole the emeralds and killed Teresa, as well as the other woman, her niece."

Bishop Murphy nodded. "Her name was Lauren Trujillo. She was a wonderful young woman. She had taken good care of Teresa in her later years. As for who could have committed such heinous acts, I've been thinking very hard about that myself."

"It's almost as if the entire situation was constructed to place Mary at the centre of events. As if someone were framing her," Annabelle said.

"It has certainly placed a lot of suspicion on Sister Mary," Bishop Murphy agreed.

"Yes," said Annabelle. "I've been racking my brains. Who would frame someone for murder? Particularly when it would have been easier to murder Teresa and steal the emeralds before we even arrived at her flat."

"The risks they took in killing Teresa whilst you were there were great. Like you say, who would do that?" the bishop wondered.

"Someone close enough to Teresa who might immediately have been suspected, perhaps?" Annabelle said. "I wonder if she had any enemies or knew someone who for really, *really* wanted those emeralds."

"That's a keen mind you have there, Annabelle. The high praise I've heard about you seems well-earned. But this is quite alarming. Until the real murderer is caught, you must protect Mary from any further plans this person may have. Keep her safe and sound. Out of harm's way."

"I most certainly will," Annabelle assured the bishop. She patted Mary's knee.

"Thank you once again, Your Excellency, for meeting with us. I am extremely indebted to you," Mary piped up.

The bishop waved Mary's compliment away. "It's the least I can do. Let me see what I can dig up about this business—and I'll also see if I can find someone else to help you with your funding."

Annabelle and Mary said their goodbyes and left the bishop dialling a number on his phone. Sara showed them out and flashed another headlight-bright smile at them before they made their way down the sunny streets of Kensington feeling much more relaxed and uplifted than they had earlier. Mary was almost skipping with joy, whilst Annabelle smiled and laughed at her friend's delight.

"Oh Annabelle, finally, we can relax! The bishop has it all in hand. Let's go to Kensington High Street, it's been so long since I've been there."

"Me too," said Annabelle. She frowned. "But shouldn't we do as the bishop says and lie low?"

"But I've not been in London for over a year! And I'll probably not return for a while either. With all this fuss, I've barely had a chance to enjoy it. This is the first time we've spent quality time together in ages. Come on, I'll buy you something."

Annabelle locked arms with Mary, and said: "Alright, you've convinced me!"

Like many areas of London, Kensington High Street had changed much over the years, but it still played host to many of London's most discerning—and richest—shoppers. Filled with one-off boutiques, antique dealers, and some of the finest chocolate and bakery shops in the British capital, the street was brimming with customers. Annabelle and Mary happily occupied themselves with window shopping.

It was Mary's turn to lead her friend, as she flitted from shop to shop as randomly as a bumble bee in spring. As good as her word, she even bought Annabelle a bag of the creamiest, sweetest fudge. Annabelle surreptitiously nibbled it as she tried to keep up with her friend.

They merrily wandered along until Mary peered into an antique shop's window. "These ornaments are astonish-oh!" Mary stood upright and stiffly turned to Annabelle. Her face was white with terror.

"I know," Annabelle said, shaking her head, "these prices *are* shocking."

"No!" Mary said, grabbing Annabelle's arm and shaking her. "I saw him!"

"Who?"

"The man in the tweed suit. The doctor. The one who ran from across the street when Lauren collapsed in front of me and then disappeared when it was obvious she was dead."

Annabelle spun around, scanning the street. "Really? Where is he?"

Mary looked around slowly, frightened by the prospect of seeing the man. "I saw his reflection in that silver mirror."

Annabelle turned back to her friend. "I'm sure it wasn't him. How could you have seen him so clearly in a mirror so small? It's just your mind playing tricks." Mary drew close to Annabelle, clutching her arm tightly. "Ow! That hurts, Mary!" Annabelle cried.

"Let's go, Annabelle. Please."

"Okay, okay. The tube station is nearby. Here, have some fudge to calm yourself down."

Mary anxiously scanned her surroundings like a hopelessly lost tourist as she and Annabelle made their way down the street. Thankfully, she didn't see the man again and when they boarded the tube, Mary relaxed. She felt safe in the carriage, but not for long.

"See?" Annabelle said, after a few minutes. "We would have seen him if he was following us."

Mary didn't reply. On turning and seeing her friend's eyes as big as full moons, Annabelle followed Mary's gaze to the window at the back of the carriage. Through the dusty, stained glass, Annabelle saw the man in a tweed suit holding onto an overhead strap.

"That's him," Mary said, her face a mask of fear.

Annabelle pushed and jostled her way through the standing passengers to get to the window. She wanted to take a closer look. It was difficult to see clearly, not least because the curvature of the rail tracks brought the man in and out of view. Eventually, she made him out. He was slim and tall, with dark skin and a brown tweed suit—much as Mary had described him.

Annabelle turned around. "Are you sure that's him?" Mary nodded and grabbed Annabelle's arm tightly. "We're safe, he can't do anything to us."

"What if he's just waiting for the right moment?" Mary said in a shaky voice. "We have to call Detective Inspector Cutcliffe."

"I agree, but you know there's no phone reception on the tube." Annabelle frowned as she thought. "I know, let's try something. I saw it in a film once. Just do as I say, okay?"

Mary nodded. "Okay."

As the train rolled to a stop at the next station, Annabelle ushered Mary to the door. She kept her eyes on the next carriage. When the doors opened with a long hiss, Annabelle stepped out of the train pulling Mary behind her. They stood in front of the train doors as people pushed and pressed past them, Annabelle's eyes searching the crowd of commuters for a sight of the tweed-suited man. At the very last moment, just before the doors closed, and with the expert timing of someone intimately familiar with London's underground transport system, Annabelle shoved Mary back onto the train. She jumped in behind her. The doors shut, and the train started pulling away.

Mary glanced around her. "Did he get off? Is he still here?"

"I don't know," replied Annabelle, "but I didn't see him. Yes, I think he's gone."

Mary allowed herself a brief sigh of relief. "Let's just go somewhere safe."

"I'll take you to my church. We'll call DI Cutcliffe on the way."

Shaking with nerves but somewhat calmed by Annabelle's forthright presence, Mary allowed herself to be taken all the way to Old Street Station, where they left the train and made their way up the escalators to the exits. As soon as they emerged into the bright sunshine, Annabelle pulled out her phone and foraged in her pockets for the card that DI Cutcliffe had given her.

"Blast! I've lost the detective inspector's number!" she said.

"No need," uttered a rough voice behind her.

Annabelle and Mary spun around and saw DI Cutcliffe standing feet away, two of his officers standing behind him as if flying in perfect formation.

"Detective Inspector Cutcliffe!" Mary exclaimed.

"We have to tell you something, Detective Inspector," Annabelle said.

Cutcliffe raised a broad hand to stop them. "There will

be plenty of time for that," he said, in an even firmer, more authoritative, and antagonistic tone than the one he usually used. Annabelle and Mary looked at each other curiously.

"Mary Willis. Annabelle Dixon," Cutcliffe continued, as his officers stepped forwards. "I am arresting you on suspicion of murder and burglary. You do not have to say anything, but it may harm your defence if you fail to mention when questioned anything which you later rely on in court. Anything you do say may be given in evidence."

CHAPTER FOURTEEN

NNABELLE STARED IN disbelief as an officer stepped forwards, gently pulled Mary's hands from her face, and placed her in handcuffs. The other officer wrapped his hand around Annabelle's wrist, but instead of complying as her friend had done, she furiously shook away his grip.

"This is utterly, astoundingly, unbelievably absurd!" she cried. "What on earth are you thinking, Detective Inspector?"

DI Cutcliffe snorted derisively. "I don't know what I was thinking earlier, allowing both of you to walk away from two separate crime scenes. My instincts were wrong on this one."

Again, Annabelle shook off the constable's repeated attempts to place her in cuffs. She glared at the officer so defiantly that he looked to Cutcliffe for direction.

"And what, may I ask, has caused this sudden turn-about? This incredible bout of folly, Detective Inspector?" Annabelle cried.

Cutcliffe didn't balk. "The right information, at the

right time, from the right person," he said, cryptically. The detective inspector nodded at the younger police officer, urging him on with the handcuffs.

Annabelle stared at Cutcliffe in disbelief. The young officer stepped forwards, hoping to catch Annabelle whilst she was stunned. Instead, Annabelle's eyes narrowed, and her almost perpetually gentle, caring face stiffened with determination. Quickly lifting up her cassock skirts, she ran.

The inspector had seen many strange sights in his decades of service. There was the elderly lady suffering from dementia who turned out to be the head of a crime syndicate, and a man who stole shop mannequins by holding them around the waist and pretending they were his girlfriends. The sight of a five-foot-eleven, sturdily built, normally self-effacing vicar sprinting into the street, her cassock flying behind her, was an entirely new occurrence, however. In flight, Annabelle had all the acceleration and natural grace of a gazelle.

Cutcliffe watched for a few seconds, frozen by the sight of Annabelle weaving through traffic, before setting off after her. "Take her to the station!" he commanded the officer holding Mary before turning to the other one. "You—come with me!"

By the time DI Cutcliffe and his fellow officer were on the move, Annabelle had already made it to the other side of the busy street. She bombed forwards with long, powerful strides and a stiff back, ducking and diving through dumbfounded crowds.

"Excuse me!"

"Sorry!"

"Move, please!"

"Vicar coming through!"

Behind Annabelle, Cutcliffe and his companion did

their best to keep up with her, but after a minute of sprinting, Cutcliffe doubled over to catch his breath.

"You okay, boss?" his fellow officer asked, slowing to a stop.

"Has she been drinking holy water or something! How the hell is she so fast? Get after her!"

The officer immediately broke into a sprint and ran off, Cutcliffe huffing and puffing behind him. "Stop that woman in the dog collar!" Cutcliffe yelled.

Annabelle reached a marketplace. She paused, swung her head from side to side with all the discernment of a guard dog then burst forwards, once more launching herself between the market stalls full of fruit and vegetables. Shoppers and stall owners, their heads twisting back and forth as if watching race cars at a track, looked on in astonishment as the galloping vicar, followed by the policemen, raced past them.

Annabelle made quite a sight as she ran and whilst Cutcliffe and the onlookers were surprised by her speed, Annabelle was not. As the tallest girl in her year for most of her school life, she was self-conscious about her height. She stood out when she wanted to fit in. To compensate, she hunched or bent her knee and always preferred sitting over standing when around her friends. When it came to sports, however, Annabelle relished her large physique. Field hockey, long-distance running, netball, or volleyball— Annabelle took to them all and grew enormously in self-confidence. Her love of cakes eventually outweighed her love of winning matches, but the endeavours of her youth had left their mark. She retained a natural athleticism she could call upon as situations demanded. She was using this strength now to outwit her pursuers.

As the chase continued, the younger officer cleverly cut

a corner by sidling between two market stalls. He gained some ground on the runaway priest. After a few more yards of sprinting, he had her in his sights. But suddenly, Annabelle flew through the air as if she were an angel spreading her wings about to rise to the heavens, her arms outstretched in front of her. "Geronimo!" she shouted. She clattered into a mass of shoppers like a bowling ball into skittles.

Behind her, the police officer quickly darted back between the stalls and into the street. He ran through the crowd towards the fallen vicar, followed seconds later by DI Cutcliffe. Annabelle was sprawled on her stomach, surrounded by shocked observers. There was barely a closed mouth among them.

"What are you playing at!?" cried the inspector when he arrived on the scene. He leant over Annabelle's cassock-clothed figure. "This is the man you want, Detective Inspector!" Annabelle gasped between heavy pants. She rolled onto her back, revealing the person she had crashed into. Staring up at Cutcliffe was the dark-skinned man in the tweed suit. "The *doctor* from the first murder!"

CHAPTER FIFTEEN

ROUGHLY AN HOUR later, DI Cutcliffe and his fellow officers marched Annabelle, Mary, and the mysterious tweed-suited man into the nearest police station.

Mary walked soberly, her head down, mouthing a silent prayer whilst the strange doctor walked gracefully behind her, his head high, his expression inscrutable. Annabelle, in contrast, had not stopped arguing from the moment she was arrested and was still voicing her astonishment at the situation.

"Terrible lack of judgement, Detective Inspector. Utterly baffling. I had you down as a good egg, someone with some common sense and decency. But this is just . . . well, it's simply . . . I'm speechless! I cannot find the words to describe the sheer absurdity of this far-fetched attempt to frame us. It's inconceivable, and yet here I am—in handcuffs! Crikey! Of all the . . ."

"Fill in the forms, please," the desk sergeant said, her voice loud and forceful enough to interrupt Annabelle's objections. Mary promptly picked up a pen and began writing down her information. Annabelle, after a few haughty sighs, did the same. The doctor, however, stared blankly ahead.

"Please fill in the forms, sir," repeated the sergeant. When the doctor showed no sign of responding, the sergeant turned to the inspector and said, "Does he speak English?"

Cutcliffe shook his head. "I have no idea."

The desk sergeant turned back to the man. "Empty your pockets," she said, slowly and loudly in the manner frequently adopted when talking to those who don't speak the national language. She put her hand in her pocket and pulled it out, splaying her fingers out wide above the desk. The man raised one eyebrow a smidgen.

"Your pocket," the inspector said, pointing at the man's trousers.

The man gave a look that could have meant he understood them but could just as easily have been a sign of defeat. He reached into his pockets, pulling out the contents. He put them on the counter.

"That goes for all of you," the desk sergeant said.

DI Cutcliffe watched closely as all three patted themselves down. The doctor was the quickest. He neatly placed a wallet, a watch, a burner phone, and an intricately engraved silver box about the size and shape of a cigarette case, on the desk in front of him.

The desk sergeant eyed the case suspiciously before picking it up and opening it. "Nice cigarette case," she said, bringing it to her nose and sniffing. She didn't smell anything—drugs nor tobacco—so she brushed a finger along the velvet insides of the case. "It's wet. Why is the inside of this cigarette case wet? And what are these?" She held up two small plastic packets. "They're cold."

The doctor continued to stare vacantly ahead, but a second after the desk sergeant posed her question, Annabelle's eyebrows rose so high, so suddenly, they almost flew off. "The ice dart!" she exclaimed. "That must be where he kept the ice darts! Those are frozen gel packs. We have them in our first aid kit at the church."

Cutcliffe nodded dismissively. "Of course you do. Empty your pockets."

The desk sergeant, DI Cutcliffe, and the strange man watched Annabelle and Mary with suspicion, then fascination. The number of objects they had secreted about themselves was extraordinary. Mary's modest and scarcely noticeable leather handbag seemed to hold enough for her to travel for days. One by one, she pulled out a passport, paperwork, two purses (one for pocket change, one for notes), a cardholder, a disposable camera, rosary beads, postcards, fridge magnets she had picked up for her friends in Africa, a Bible, some hard-boiled sweets, and finally, the clear bag which contained the foil-wrapped cake given to her by Teresa.

Annabelle's treasure trove was no less impressive. After pulling out her own Bible from her cassock pocket and taking off her watch, she placed on the counter her mobile phone, a bus pass, a notebook, a pencil, a packet of wet wipes, mints, a now empty bag of fudge, lip balm, a purse, a bunch of keys, various crumpled receipts and sweet wrappers, a hairbrush, a sewing kit, and then finally, her own bag of cake.

"Are you finished?" the desk sergeant asked. She sounded exasperated. "We must dispose of the foodstuff, I'm afraid." After putting the items in boxes, she pointed to Annabelle and Mary's identical bags. "Mind telling me what those are?"

"They're slices of cake," Annabelle retorted, picking hers up from the desk and opening the zipper across the top of the bag. "And if you don't mind, I'd rather you didn't dispose of them. They were gifts from a very kind old lady. Now deceased, unfortunately."

As Annabelle unfolded the foil to reveal the cake, remarkably well-preserved despite its travels around London, the desk sergeant shot DI Cutcliffe an alarmed look. "Is that okay, sir?" she asked him. He replied with a shrug and a defeated shake of his head. "Let them eat cake," he said. He let out a hard, humourless laugh.

The sergeant, who by this point had indulged the trio far more than was typical, pursed her lips and continued to pack boxes with their personal effects. Whilst she did so, DI Cutcliffe persevered with the doctor's forms. The doctor was still staring at some distant spot on the opposite wall.

With this backdrop, her irritation over the turn that the day's events had taken showing on her face, Annabelle slowly brought the slice of cake to her mouth. She was determined to enjoy it, especially as this might be her last piece of cake for a while. She took a large, haughty bite. "Ow!" she cried, immediately spraying cake all over the desk. She clutched the side of her jaw.

Everyone turned to see crumbs spray everywhere. There was a loud tinkling sound. Pairs of eyes took in Annabelle's pained expression and then roamed the scraps of cake scattered across the counter. Astonishingly, there among the crumbs, were two marble-sized gems that caught the light despite the sugary remnants of chocolate sponge and mousse that clung to them.

Still holding her jaw, Annabelle slowly lowered the rest of the cake onto the table. She broke it apart, revealing another four gems.

"The Cats-Eye emeralds!" she said, mumbling through tooth pain. "Teresa baked them into the cakes!"

The desk sergeant lifted Mary's cake from its bag and tore off the wrapping. On pulling it apart, she found another six brilliant jewels.

Cutcliffe snorted. "I have to say, Reverend, this is one hell of an act you've put up, but you're only confirming what we already know. Your friend here, with you as an accomplice, committed murder in order to steal some of the most valuable jewels ever to have reached these shores."

"But I . . ."

"You'd have been better off letting those cakes go into the rubbish. We'd never have found them." Cutcliffe waved Annabelle away. "Put her in a cell and the doctor in another," the inspector commanded. "Mary Willis, come with me. It's time you told the truth."

DI Cutcliffe was a formidable interviewer. He was not the most adaptable nor even the most perceptive. Some said his technique was rather old-fashioned. But he was by far the most detailed, and by an even further stretch, the most determined inquisitor any unfortunate reprobate was likely to meet. After ten minutes of questioning Mary without gaining any new information, he got tough. When that didn't work, he paced furiously up and down the interview room. That only seemed to make Mary cry. The inspector began to worry. Cutcliffe hated two things more than anything in the world—criminals and the sound of women crying. When the two things came in one package, he could barely stand it.

"Look, Sister Mary," he said, after giving her enough

time to stifle her sobs and wipe her face, "you've told me the same story about a dozen times over. You can cry all you want, but I know it isn't the truth."

"It is!" Mary said, a shake in her voice suggesting that she was close to breaking down again.

The inspector sat at the table, leant forwards, and struggled to contort his face into the warmest, friendliest expression he could muster. It took him a while. "Look at it from my perspective," he said. "You're asking me to believe in an almost insane number of coincidences, flukes, and mishaps."

Cutcliffe reeled off a list of accusations, counting them one by one on his fingers. "First, you claim that Lauren Trujillo after arranging to meet you, died at your feet, but you don't know who killed her or how. Second, you claim you *forgot* to hand me a crucial piece of evidence, the note. Third, when you realised you had it, instead of handing it over, you kept it to yourself because it seemed the *smartest thing to do*. Fourth, only you and your friend were with Teresa Nortega when she was killed. Fifth, immediately afterwards, her flat is apparently ransacked, but you say this happened after you left. And six, missing emeralds owned by Ms. Nortega are found baked into slices of cake that are on your person, yet you deny all knowledge of their existence. Now, just think about how that sounds. That's a hell of a lot of convenient accidents."

Mary looked up, her eyes red and her nose runny from crying. She laughed despairingly. "But it's true. Accidents are the story of my life." The inspector sighed and left the interview room, still shaking his head.

"Sir?" the young officer who had been waiting outside said to him. "Did you find anything out?"

"She's either the greatest liar I've ever met," DI Cutcliffe replied, "or she's telling the truth."

"But she can't be telling the truth, sir. If she didn't do it, who did?"

Cutcliffe looked into his young officer's eyes. "It's a good thing we brought in two suspects, although I was rather hoping I wouldn't have to question the other one."

"Why's that, sir?"

"She talks even faster than she runs."

CHAPTER SIXTEEN

D I CUTCLIFFE AND his fellow officer entered the interview room. Annabelle was deep in thought.

"Detective Inspector!" she said after a pause. "I've been wanting to speak to you for hours now!"

Cutcliffe exchanged an 'I told you so' look with his accompanying officer. "This is PC Montgomery. He'll be sitting in on the interview."

"Of course," Annabelle said graciously. "Be my guest."

The policemen squinted at her before taking their seats. Cutcliffe pressed the 'on' button of the tape machine and introduced the interview with a record of the time, date, and persons present. When he finished, he turned his attention to Annabelle and spoke in a deep, confident voice. "Reverend Dixon, we've placed you at both crime scenes, we've discovered that you concealed evidence, and we've caught you with stolen property. This is an open-and-shut case, frankly. All you have to decide is how easy you want this to go."

Annabelle leant forwards and pointed her finger at

Cutcliffe who peered, frowning, at its tip. "I'm forming a theory," she countered, oblivious to the inspector's accusatory tone. "The pieces make little sense on their own, but when you put them all together, they fit as perfectly as, well, a jigsaw."

"You have a theory, do you?" the inspector said. He sighed, sat back in his chair, and folded his arms over his stomach.

"Oh yes, I do."

"Why am I not surprised? Does this theory still involve darts of poisoned ice and emeralds as cake ingredients? Or is it something more plausible, like mind control? Invisibility cloaks, perhaps? Transfiguration, even?"

"I know you suspect me, Detective Inspector," Annabelle said, smiling wryly as if this was a tense game of Scrabble and not an interrogation, "but if this was an *open-and-shut* case, as you say, then how do you explain the doctor following us?"

"He could be anyone!" the inspector blurted out. "A random passer-by who was unfortunate enough to land in— or be landed on, I should say—this mess."

"Not a random passer-by at all, Detective Inspector," Annabelle said, raising her finger as if scoring a point. "He fits the description Mary gave you at the first crime scene exactly. Tweed suit. Waistcoat. Brown leather shoes."

"Reverend, this is London. It has a population of over nine million people. I could tell my officers to find me an albino in a pink dress, and they would find one by lunchtime."

"It's still strange that he was in the vicinity at the time you arrested us, don't you think?" Annabelle replied. "And though you scoff at the ice dart theory, what could be stranger than an empty cigarette case that is wet on the inside, even though it has not rained for days now? And don't forget the frozen gel packs!" Cutcliffe, still sitting back in his chair, pursed his lips.

Annabelle continued. "I'd also fashion a guess that the toxicology reports on Teresa showed that poison entered her bloodstream directly. Perhaps via a needle or possibly by *a dart*. I presume you are suggesting that we killed the two women by making them drink a toxic substance. You would be wrong with that assumption. There was no time for it."

"There is a grey area surrounding how you poisoned both of them, I grant you," the inspector said. "The toxicology reports are inconclusive."

Annabelle smiled at Cutcliffe's answer. "If I'm not mistaken, Detective Inspector, you reason that we murdered Teresa, turned over her flat to find the emeralds, and then baked them into a cake so that we could carry them around without anyone knowing."

"Precisely," Cutcliffe scowled.

"But how, Detective Inspector, would we have had the time to bake such a delicious cake, with those complex, rich flavours, in such little time? There were two hours, if that, between leaving you at the first crime scene and our meeting at the second. You can check the closed-circuit television cameras at the tube stations. It took us over an hour to arrive at Teresa's flat."

"That gives you plenty of time," Cutcliffe responded.

"If anyone who likes to bake heard you say that, Detective Inspector, they would laugh. Laugh, I tell you! That cake is full of cream and fine melted chocolate mixed extremely slowly to prevent curdling. It has flecks of almonds that were toasted gently to bring out their flavour. The cake was beautifully moist—that could only have come about from the cake being cooked slowly on a low heat. Two of the finest chefs in the world couldn't bake such a cake in less than three hours!" Annabelle's voice rose as if she were enunciating a dramatic monologue. "There's only one conclusion to come to, Detective Inspector. Teresa's cake was baked before we got there!"

"Maybe so!" the inspector said, angrily slamming his palm on the table. "But you still stole it!"

"Why would we upturn the entire flat to look for the emeralds if we knew they were in the cake? We would have simply taken it from the kitchen." Annabelle slammed her own palm on the table. "Which is where cakes should be when they are not in people's tummies!"

"This is insanity! We're here to interview you, Reverend! Not the other way around!" DI Cutcliffe stood and paced across the room. "Here we are, investigating a double murder case and a theft amounting to millions of pounds whilst you squawk about bloody cakes!"

PC Montgomery hunched over and focused on his hands. He hadn't attended many interviews and when he heard that he was to attend this one, he expected to observe a routine cross-examination, not a confrontation between two boiling, blustering firebrands.

"You're a Catholic man, aren't you, Detective Inspector?" said Annabelle.

"What does that have to do with anything?"

"That's why you gave Sister Mary the benefit of the doubt initially, and that's why . . ."

The two policemen looked at Annabelle as she trailed off.

"What?" PC Montgomery ventured, in a quiet, shaky voice.

Annabelle looked to the side, deep in thought again. Her face changed, and she nodded to herself as if struck by a stunning revelation. She turned her face back to the inspector, her eyes full of righteousness.

"That's why you trust the bishop implicitly."

DI Cutcliffe stared at her. Slowly, he took his seat again and spoke in a low tone. "What are you implying, Reverend?"

"I would bet the entire value of those emeralds," Annabelle said, "that it was the bishop who told you to arrest us today. And who told you precisely where we would be."

DI Cutcliffe's pupils contracted to pinpoints. "So what if it was?"

"It should be obvious, Detective Inspector," Annabelle said slowly. She pressed her finger into the tabletop for emphasis. "The bishop is behind it *all*."

CHAPTER SEVENTEEN

"THAT'S A BOLD claim," Cutcliffe said, after taking a moment to make sure Annabelle had said what he thought she had. "I underestimated you. You topped the ice dart theory. If you're trying to get off with an insanity plea, you're doing an excellent job."

"Like it or not, Detective Inspector, it's the truth," Annabelle said, raising her chin.

"I don't suppose you have any evidence to back up your claim?"

"Oh, I do. It's all right under our noses."

The inspector raised his eyebrows, unable to find words to respond to something he found so extraordinary.

"I've been thinking about our meeting with Teresa since it happened," began Annabelle. "She said she liked to sit by the window to keep watch. Not to *look outside* or to *see people*, but to *keep watch*, as if on guard. As she died, she was in the middle of saying something about being in danger, just like in the note delivered to Mary by the woman at the café."

"Could just be a turn of phrase. Probably means nothing," Cutcliffe said.

"But they were her dying words . . . Put all these points together with the fact that Teresa had hidden the emeralds in a cake, and it suggests she felt watched, observed, even in her home, and not by a benevolent person for a harmless reason. Only a powerful person could intimidate like that—someone with spies, accomplices, a large network, and employees. Someone as powerful as the bishop."

"I'll indulge you for a moment and agree that it sounds like someone was watching them. Teresa's niece obviously felt frightened enough to write that note. But why the bishop? There's no connection."

"Think about it, Detective Inspector. The bishop has known everything from the start. He told Mary and me that he called you after he had learnt about Teresa's death. He called me multiple times at the church on the same day. From whom would he have learnt about the murder so quickly and that we were at the scene, if not the killer himself? And wasn't it the bishop who told you where to find us? I'm guessing he gave you a clever excuse as to how he knew, but how *did* he know where we were if the tweed-suited man was not following us on his orders?"

"Harrumph." Cutliffe frowned.

"Consider this, Detective Inspector, if Teresa were in danger, why would she contact Mary for help? Why not the police? Or indeed, why not the bishop himself, if they were as friendly as he claims?"

"Maybe it wasn't serious enough."

"Or maybe she knew that no one would believe her."

Cutcliffe sighed and looked to his officer, who shrugged his shoulders, his long face like that of a sleepy bloodhound.

"Okay, so Teresa was in danger. Why not leave and get to safety? Why stay in her flat?"

"I believe there are two reasons for that, Detective Inspector. First, Teresa rarely left her home. She had a limp and mentioned that her niece performed most tasks for her. Second, I don't think even Teresa realised the depths to which the bishop would sink. She wanted to guard against the theft of the emeralds but had no idea that the bishop was willing to kill for them. It certainly shocked her when we told her about the death of her niece."

DI Cutcliffe put his hands on the table and leant forwards. He was visibly struggling with what Annabelle was saying. It made sense, but it was still too far-fetched for him.

"So these . . . 'Cat emeralds' . . . ."

"Cats-Eye emeralds," Annabelle corrected.

"Cats-Eye emeralds," the detective inspector tried again. "Why give them to you? Why not give them to her niece to stuff somewhere safe? Why not put them somewhere meant for valuable things? A bank deposit box or a museum vault?"

Annabelle nodded at the legitimacy of the question. "I think Teresa very much wanted to help Mary and considered her above reproach. I don't know if Teresa suspected the bishop, but she knew that whoever she gave the emeralds to would be in grave danger. Perhaps Teresa hatched a plan to give them to Mary because no one would suspect her of having them, especially if Mary were carrying them unwittingly. Perhaps it was Teresa's way of helping Mary with her funding."

Annabelle paused her finger to her lips. She thought for a moment before speaking again. "Or, had she not died so suddenly, Teresa might have given us instructions—no doubt cryptic—on what we were to do with them. Perhaps she would have told us to meet someone else who could help sell them, or hide them, or maybe even warn us against contacting the bishop or people within the church, if she suspected them. Either way, it would seem Teresa saw Mary as a safe haven for her jewels."

There were a few moments of silence as the detective inspector leant back and scratched his head furiously whilst he turned over Annabelle's theories in his cluttered mind. Eventually, he sighed, shook his head, and said, "I'm sorry, Reverend. It's not enough."

"What do you mean?" Annabelle replied. She almost wailed.

"It's pure conjecture. There's not enough hard evidence for me to do anything. I will not bang on the bishop's door and start throwing accusations around based on nothing but daydreams even if you are a woman of the cloth."

Annabelle pursed her lips. She may have jutted out her lower jaw a little. "Then let me talk to the bishop!" she said.

Cutcliffe chuckled. "Not a chance!"

"It's the only way!" Annabelle persisted. "Right now, the bishop must believe that Mary and I have the emeralds. The entire reason he made you arrest us was a last-ditch attempt to discover where we had hidden them. If you let me call him now and tell him I'm willing to cut a deal, I assure you he'll do exactly what I tell him."

"You're being ridiculous!" Cutcliffe bellowed. "Do you expect me to allow you to bother the bishop with these crazy ideas of yours?"

"I'm willing to stake my entire reputation on this, Detective Inspector. You can listen in whilst I talk to him, and if it turns out that the bishop is innocent, I'll sign any confession you like." Annabelle was excited by her idea.

"And I won't say another word about it," she added. She drew her forefinger and thumb across her mouth as if zipping it shut.

Cutcliffe chuckled darkly at the bizarre turn the interview had taken. "You do realise," he said, with a note of defeat in his voice, "that what you're asking me to go along with is highly illegal *and* insane."

"I believe her." Cutcliffe and Annabelle turned to PC Montgomery. They had both completely forgotten that he was in the room.

Annabelle smiled triumphantly. The inspector rubbed a broad hand across his face. He glanced at the vicar's unyielding expression and then at the equally adamant PC Montgomery. Slowly, he pressed "stop" on the tape recorder, ejected the tape, and put it in his pocket.

"Make sure the coast is clear, Montgomery. We'd better leave through the back entrance," he said in an almost inaudible voice. "You better be right about this, Reverend, or I'll be saying Hail Marys for the rest of my life."

CHAPTER EIGHTEEN

BARELY TEN MINUTES later, Reverend Annabelle, DI Cutcliffe, and PC Montgomery were zooming across London in an unmarked police car. They were headed to Kensington. Annabelle had made the call to the bishop's office requesting a meeting. She had said little apart from a sly reference to "a deal." Unsurprisingly, Sara claimed that Bishop Murphy was immediately available.

"I can't believe I'm doing this," DI Cutcliffe muttered to himself once he had parked the car in a discreet spot a little way down from the bishop's house.

Annabelle shifted in her seat. She was breathing deeply, feeling exhilarated and increasingly nervous.

"Now listen to me," Cutcliffe said. "These are the rules. Don't, whatever you do, mention anything about me. If this blows up, I don't want anyone to know I'm the one who allowed a cake-obsessed vicar from East London to conduct a sting operation to entrap a bent bishop. Got it?"

"Oh, of course, I mean . . ."

"And get him to talk," the inspector added. "Get him to

confirm what you're saying. We need him to incriminate himself or at least tell us some things that we can use as evidence."

"Yes," Annabelle said, almost literally biting her tongue.

"And . . ." Cutcliffe looked from Annabelle to Montgomery and back again, "don't be nervous. I don't usually say this kind of thing to suspects, but I wouldn't be here if I didn't think you were on to something."

Annabelle seemed to relax at this display of trust, however meagre. "Thank you, Detective Inspector. I won't let you down."

"I hope not. Okay, call my phone. Put yours on speaker. We'll mute ours so you don't hear us. When you've walked down the street a way, I want you to say a few words and then turn to look back at us. If we can hear you we'll give you a thumbs up. If we give you a thumbs down, come straight back to the car. We'll figure something else out."

"Right," Annabelle said. She was furiously shredding a tissue between her fingers.

"Once you're inside and the bishop has said enough, we'll enter his mansion," DI Cutcliffe continued. "If we don't like what you're doing, we'll enter and arrest you again. If things turn unsafe, we'll enter. Got that? Whatever happens, we'll enter."

Annabelle nodded. "Yes."

"Okay. Time to go. Call my phone."

Annabelle rang Cutcliffe and placed the call on speaker. She gave one last nod to Cutcliffe and Montgomery. They nodded back, inhaling deeply, their nostrils flaring as they sought to keep their emotions in check. They were like parents sending their firstborn off to school for the first time. They were brimming with support, pride, and sadness, knowing that their job was done for now and that the outcome was in Annabelle's hands. PC Montgomery clutched a fist to his lips.

Annabelle got out of the car. She looked around and began walking down the street. "Um . . . ah . . . oh, I'm terrible at things like this. I feel like a madman talking to myself in the street. Ah . . . is that okay?" Annabelle turned back to see the inspector give her a thumbs up. "Okay. Good. Well, off I go. Oh, I suppose I should stop talking," she said, turning again to see the inspector give her another thumbs up. "Yes, well . . . good."

Annabelle ambled towards the bishop's residence. She walked up the path to the door with the brass knocker. At the top of the steps, Annabelle paused. The vicar shook her limbs, stood up straight, and composed herself. She was aiming for indifference, tossing her hair back for good measure. Then she knocked.

The door opened. "Hello, Reverend," Sara said in her still unplaceable accent. She stepped aside and waved Annabelle in. "Bishop Murphy is waiting for you in his office."

"Ah, good," Annabelle said, as casually as she could manage. She strode to the office door, placed a hand on the doorknob, and looked back at Sara.

"Please go right in," Sara said. Annabelle took a deep breath and opened the door.

"Reverend Annabelle!" Bishop Murphy said in his very placeable Irish accent. He stood up from his desk and walked around it to greet her. "A pleasant—and somewhat unexpected—surprise!" He shook Annabelle's hand whilst she looked away dismissively.

"Yes," she said, "I suppose."

The bishop returned to his chair whilst Annabelle took one opposite. She crossed her legs in what she thought would be an elegant movement full of ease and grace but found the position so uncomfortable that she quickly shuffled her legs to uncross them.

"So what brings you here, Reverend?" Bishop Murphy asked with a wry smile.

"Well, I have something that you want. And I want to see how far you'll go to get it."

CHAPTER NINETEEN

THE BISHOP RAISED a curious eyebrow.

"Oh, gosh!" Annabelle exclaimed suddenly. "That sounds awfully flirty, doesn't it? Well, I don't mean that!" She laughed awkwardly. "I'm talking about the emeralds. The Cats-Eye emeralds. I'm saying that I have them, and, well . . ."

Annabelle trailed off in a series of stammers and snorted laughs. The bishop watched her, amusement lighting up his eyes, his lips twisted by a smirk.

After Annabelle had stopped hemming and hawing, there was a pause before the bishop spoke. "What makes you think I'm interested in the emeralds?"

Annabelle gulped. Was Bishop Murphy going to pretend he didn't care about the jewels? Did he know this was a trap?

Annabelle sat up straight and regained some of her composure. "Well, you said that the emeralds were exhibited privately and that only prominent collectors were even aware of them. So for you to have known about the jewels, it was likely that you were one of those collectors. When we visited earlier, Sara told us about the precious items that you have in the cellar below."

The bishop laughed gently. "That's true. I do have a rather excellent collection of artefacts. That doesn't necessarily mean I'm interested in the emeralds, though."

Annabelle shifted uncomfortably on her seat again. A note of doubt entered her mind. She gazed around the room as if some support could be found there, but deep down she knew that she was on her own. Now or never, she thought.

"I must be mistaken then," she said, placing her hands on the chair's armrests to push herself to stand. "I had thought you would be interested in a deal. I suppose I'll just have to find someone else. Someone with better taste."

"Sit down, Reverend," the bishop said sharply. He dropped his smile, replacing it with a sneer. "Of course, I'm interested." Annabelle sat back down.

"But how do I know you have them? Can you prove it?" he said.

Annabelle eyes met the bishop's. She laughed loudly. "Do you really think I'd bring them with me? Here? Ha! I've seen how far you're willing to go to get them, Bishop, and I was rather hoping to have my tea tonight in one piece!"

The bishop's sneer transformed into a sly grin. "Clever. But I'm not sure what you're implying, Reverend. I'm merely an interested collector."

"Tosh!" Annabelle exclaimed. "We both know that you've gone out of your way to get your hands on those emeralds!"

"Do we?"

"When Teresa rejected *your* inquiries, you decided to steal them and have Sister Mary take the blame. You put Mary in touch with Teresa and waited for the perfect opportunity to steal the emeralds whilst setting up Mary as the prime suspect. You underestimated Teresa and her niece, however, didn't you?"

Annabelle continued. "Teresa, possibly suspecting something, arranged for her niece, Lauren, to meet Mary in a public space. On her way there, Lauren realised she was being spied upon. In case anything happened to her, Lauren wrote a note to point to the fact that Teresa was in danger. You ordered your assassin to kill Lauren before she could reveal anything, but she managed to hand the note to Mary just before she died."

"An interesting perspective," the bishop smirked.

Annabelle waited for him to say more, and when he didn't, she carried on. "The perfect chance soon presented itself, however, when instead of going to the authorities with the note, Mary and I went to Teresa's house. Your hired assassin, presented with this gift, killed Teresa with us right next to her. He planned to wait for us to leave, then enter the flat, find the emeralds, and steal them, leaving us to take the blame. The good news was that we left immediately, the bad news was that we took the emeralds with us.

"After your assassin searched Teresa's flat and found nothing, you realised that we had got the emeralds. At a loss, you tried the direct approach. You contacted us to arrange a meeting to discern what we were up to and where the emeralds were. How am I doing, Bishop Murphy? Am I right or am I right?"

CHAPTER TWENTY

BISHOP MURPHY BOWED his head. His hands were steepled in front of him. The large ruby ring on his left hand glinted in the sunlight.

"I suspected that Teresa had somehow given you the emeralds or at least a clue as to where they were, but you seemed entirely ignorant of the affair when we spoke," the bishop said.

"At the time, we didn't even know we had them," Annabelle replied.

"Leaving me with two choices: To kill you and hope that you had them on you, or to follow you until I found out more."

"But if you killed us and we didn't have them, you'd have lost the only chance of finding them."

"It was a conundrum, to be sure," Bishop Murphy said. "But there's one thing I never told you. Those emeralds originate from West Africa. I was sure Teresa wanted Mary to have them so that she could sell them and fund her hospital there. A sense of justice and charity was always Teresa's biggest weakness. It's the reason her ex-husband was so generous as to give the emeralds to her. I was certain you had them. I just didn't know where you had secreted them.

"And you, Reverend, were getting a little too close to home. You suspected that someone was framing Mary, and you knew that I was the one who had put her in contact with Teresa. Not only did you have the emeralds I wanted, but you were a day or two away from implicating me. If it was just Mary, as I had planned, I wouldn't have been afraid, but you," he pointed a finger at Annabelle and looked down the length of it as if aiming a gun, "you were sure to cause me a lot of trouble. I was certain of it."

Annabelle matched the bishop's flinty, shrewd glare. "So after speaking to us, you called DI Cutcliffe and told him you were suspicious. You hoped that he would find out what we didn't even know ourselves—the location of the emeralds."

The bishop opened his hands in mock-apology. "I'm good with Cutcliffe. Once he discovered the emeralds, I could have easily persuaded him that they were my property. At the very least, I would know they were safe, and I'd have had a head-start on what the police planned to do with them once they took them from you. Better that the jewels were in police custody than in the unpredictable hands of two religious women who didn't even know what they had. Which makes me wonder, Reverend, how are you sitting here with me when you should be locked up?"

Annabelle squirmed in her seat. "I blamed Mary," she said. She found it difficult to even say the words, but she gave Bishop Murphy a brief, sly smile. "She was, after all, intended to take the blame for the murders your assassin committed, wasn't she?"

The bishop chuckled. "Very clever, Reverend. Very

clever, indeed. You are as merciless and as canny a player of games as I. You will make a very intriguing vicar. Now," he said, slapping his hands on the table, "let's talk numbers, shall we?"

Annabelle balked. Though he had insinuated plenty, the bishop hadn't actually confessed to anything. Was this enough for DI Cutcliffe? Was it too late? She searched for something she could say which would force the bishop to reply with a definitive answer, but Bishop Murphy was gazing at her directly, waiting for her answer to his question.

"Ah . . . well . . . what are the lives of two women worth?"

"You tell me, Reverend."

"Um . . ." Annabelle tried to think of a number that didn't sound too preposterous. "Ten million pounds?"

The bishop's face dropped, and his jaw slackened before he broke into such a fit of laughter he almost fell off his chair.

"Ten?! Haha! Ten million pounds?! Hahahahaha!" he bellowed, wiping tears from his eyes. "Oh dear me!"

"Is that too much?" Annabelle asked in a small voice.

Her comment initiated another fit of laughter that was louder than the first. "Stop! Stop it! Hahahahahahahaha-ha!" the bishop cried, struggling to calm himself. "Annabelle! Ten million is less than I spend on travel in a year! I had two women killed in cold blood for those baubles! I pulled in favours with a respected detective, albeit he was too stupid to know why. I got myself involved with a professional killer! I risked my neck! You think all that is worth a measly ten million? Ha! Why, I'm almost insulted!"

"Twenty million?" Annabelle blurted out.

"Ha!" the bishop cried. "I'll give you fifteen million and

a piece of advice—get someone better to do your negotiating in future."

"Fifty! Fifty million!" yelled Annabelle as the door burst open with a loud crash.

Bishop Murphy leapt out of his chair and onto the balls of his feet. He had the agility of a cat. DI Cutcliffe and PC Montgomery stormed into the office. They each took a side of the room and cornered Bishop Murphy behind his desk, where PC Montgomery grabbed his hands and placed him in cuffs.

"What's going on here?" Bishop Murphy cried.

"You're being arrested for murder and theft, Bishop," Cutcliffe said grimly.

"You do not have to say anything, but it may harm your defence if you fail to mention when questioned anything which you later rely on in court. Anything you do say may be given in evidence." PC Montgomery's eyes were shining. It was his first arrest. He was delighted it was in relation to such a high profile case. His mum would be so proud.

"Surely not one hundred million?" Annabelle said, still caught up in her bidding war.

"Cutcliffe!" the bishop shouted. "You're not going to let this happen, are you?"

"Unlike you, Bishop, I'm compelled to act when I hear a confession," Cutcliffe said.

Bishop Murphy turned his head to Annabelle, his eyes blazing. "You! You tricked me!"

"Come on, Bishop Murphy, we've got a lot to talk about. See you down the station," Cutcliffe said. Montgomery guided the bishop out of the room as he snarled and squirmed under the constable's grip.

Left alone in the bishop's office, DI Cutcliffe and Annabelle looked at each other. Cutcliffe sighed and patted

Annabelle on the shoulder. "You did a respectable job, Reverend. The bishop is one hell of a slippery customer. Too slippery for his own good, some would say."

"Thank you, Inspector," Annabelle said, dizzy with excitement and adrenaline. "I'm just glad it's all over. Can I go to the station to meet Mary?"

"I'll put in a call for her to be released from custody."

"Will I be able to pick up my belongings?"

"Of course," the inspector said. "I'll have the desk sergeant have them ready for you."

"Excellent, and one more thing, Detective Inspector," Annabelle said, causing the inspector to stifle a sigh and raise an eyebrow. "You didn't really throw away Teresa's cake, did you?"

EPILOGUE

"OOH! LOOK AT this, Cecilia . . ." Annabelle shook the newspaper out.

'Further thefts revealed in ongoing Bishop Murphy case.'

"There's an entire two-page spread of all the things that man has stolen over the years."

Annabelle lay the newspaper over the kitchen table. Cecilia turned away from the steaming beef Wellington she was carefully slicing to look at it.

"Oh, my! There's more gold in that haul than in the Tower of London!" Annabelle said as she perused photos of the shiny trinkets and ancient artefacts found in Bishop Murphy's cellar. "Whatever did he want with so much jewellery? Was he going to wear it?" Annabelle giggled before continuing to read.

"'Murphy's closest accomplice is still unnamed and refuses to talk. It is

```
believed, however, that the man has been
  involved in at least four other major
  thefts, in addition to committing two
                murders.'"
```

"Isn't that astonishing?"

Before Cecilia could answer, the heavy clomping of Father John's boots sounded in the church hallway. He entered the kitchen, inhaled deeply, and smiled at Cecilia.

"The church's best kept secret strikes again! This smells delicious, Cecilia," he said.

Mary was close behind him. She agreed. "It smells utterly splendid! Hello, Cecilia, Annabelle."

"Mary! I was just reading the day's report on the case. Have you seen this?" Annabelle said, holding up the paper as Mary and Father John took their seats.

"Oh, Annabelle, I've had just about all I can handle regarding the entire affair," Mary replied.

Father John shot her a quick look. "Have you not heard the news, Mary?" Mary's nonplussed gaze told him she hadn't.

"Hand me that paper, would you, Annabelle? Now, let me see," he said, noisily turning pages. "Ah! Here it is."

```
"'São Paulo, Brazil: Albert Trujillo was
 astonished to discover that following the
tragic death of his aunt, Teresa Nortega, he
  was to inherit Ms. Nortega's collection of
   jewels. The collection includes the famed
   Cats-Eye emeralds. In a statement given to
    journalists two days ago, Albert Trujillo
announced that he believed that his aunt had
```

intended to sell the emeralds. He further
stated he would heed the calls to follow her
wishes and put the jewels up for auction at
Sotheby's in London. The monies raised from
the sale will be donated in their entirety to
the Saint Baptiste hospital of West Africa.'"

Mary gasped, her hand shooting to her mouth.

"Why, that's wonderful!" Annabelle said.

"You'll be a hero when you go back to Africa," Cecilia added, as she brought the plates of beef wrapped in puff pastry to the table.

"I don't . . . that's incredible . . . is it really true?" Mary stuttered.

"Says so right here," Father John added, handing the newspaper into Annabelle's eager hands. "Come on, plenty of time for talk later, let's eat now."

Cecilia sat and, with everyone silent, Father John blessed the food. As soon as he finished, the air filled with a chorus of cutlery and appreciative moans as they took their first bites.

"Expected to go for one hundred and *fifty-seven million* pounds!" Annabelle shouted, suddenly. The others looked up. "I was going to sell them for ten!" Mary, Father John, and Cecilia exchanged glances. "Oh, never mind," Annabelle said, tossing the paper aside and tucking into her food.

They ate heartily, enjoying the delicious meal, pleasant company, and easy conversation. Father John's humour, Cecilia's compassion, and Annabelle's non-stop chatter distracted even Mary, who was in shock.

The meat course was followed by sweet, fruity, juicy

jam turnovers—a specialty of Cecilia's. "These are divine, Cecilia!" Annabelle said.

Their hunger satisfied, they basked in the afterglow of a tasty, filling meal. Annabelle took a long sip of water. "Father, I have something I've been meaning to talk to you about."

"Oh? Of course. What is it?"

"Well," Annabelle began, taking the time to think about her words, "St. Clement's is a truly wonderful church. And you are undoubtedly the best person I could possibly have had to help me during my first assignment. I've loved every moment of our work here, and despite all the fuss and difficulties, I would not exchange these experiences for anything." Father John sighed. He was old enough and experienced enough to know what was coming.

"But I find myself yearning for the green fields and changing seasons of the country," Annabelle continued. "When I thought about what it would be like to practice, I always envisaged serving a small, rural community. Even though I grew up here, in East London, I feel somewhat misplaced now, as a priest."

"Annabelle," Father John said, "I thought you would be misplaced here too, honestly. When I first saw you, I thought the work would eat you alive! But having worked with you as much as I have, I can say without a doubt that I can think of no one finer, no one more accomplished, with whom I'd rather work. You've performed miracles in your parish. You've reached people many of your predecessors had given up on. You've grown the congregation at a time when every other church in London is struggling just to maintain its numbers. Why, I believe I've learnt more from you than I've helped you."

"Thank you, Father, I appreciate the kind words."

Annabelle smiled. "I'm sorry to be saying this, as I will dearly miss you and Cecilia, and indeed the community. But . . ."

"Say no more." Father John raised his hand. "I understand, Annabelle. Let me talk to the archbishop. I'll see what I can do. I can't guarantee anything, and almost certainly not soon, but I'll do my best."

Annabelle felt touched and smiled with gratitude. "Thank you, that would be lovely."

"Annabelle, are you really thinking about leaving? We will miss you so much," Cecilia said, sorrow clear in her eyes.

Annabelle shrugged apologetically. Father John raised his glass of red wine, prompting the others to do the same.

"Let's not think of this as a reason to be sad, but rather, a cause to be glad that we had Annabelle for as long as we did," he said. "Let's be grateful for this breath of fresh air amidst the smog of London and wish Annabelle a pleasant journey wherever she goes!"

They clinked their glasses. "Cheers!"

"There will be adventures, Annabelle," Mary said.

"I know," Annabelle replied. "I can't wait." She sipped her wine, her eyes shining with anticipation. Adventures were what she lived for.

Thank you for reading *Death at the Cafe*! I hope you love Annabelle as much as I do. Her story continues in *Murder at the Mansion*. Does she get her heart's desire?

A madcap lady vicar. A mansion of mayhem. And a murder more diabolical than devil's food cake...

Trouble arises when Annabelle welcomes a new resi-

dent to her quaint parish. But instead of a chat over tea and cake, Annabelle is served a heaping plate of murder, and another helping of handsome Inspector Mike Nicholls!

Can Annabelle achieve what the authorities cannot and solve the murder? And what will the inspector make of her involvement? Order Murder at the Mansion from Amazon and find out! Murder at the Mansion is FREE in Kindle Unlimited.

To find out about new books, sign up for my newsletter: https://www.alisongolden.com

If you love the Reverend Annabelle series, you'll want to read the *USA Today* bestselling Inspector Graham series featuring a new and unusual detective with a phenomenal memory and a tragic past. The first in the series, *The Case of the Screaming Beauty* is available for purchase from Amazon

and FREE in Kindle Unlimited. *The Case of the Screaming Beauty* also comes for free as part of my starter library available to subscribers of my newsletter.

And don't miss the Roxy Reinhardt mysteries. Will Roxy triumph after her life falls apart? She's sacked from her job, her boyfriend dumps her, she's out of money. So, on a whim, she goes on the trip of a lifetime to New Orleans, There, she gets mixed up in a Mardi Gras murder. *Things were going to be fine. They were,*

weren't they? Get the first in the series, Mardi Gras Madness from Amazon. Also FREE in Kindle Unlimited!

If you're looking for something edgy and dangerous, root for Diana Hunter as she seeks justice after a devastating crime destroys her family. Start following her journey in this non-stop series of suspense and action. The first book in the series, Snatched is available to buy on Amazon and is FREE in Kindle Unlimited.

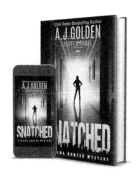

I hugely appreciate your help in spreading the word about *Death at the Cafe*, including telling a friend. Reviews help readers find books! Please leave a review on your favourite book site.

Turn the page for an excerpt from the next book in the Reverend Annabelle series, *Murder at the Mansion* . . .

A Reverend
Annabelle Dixon
Mystery

murder
at the
mansion

ALISON GOLDEN
JAMIE VOUGEOT

MURDER AT THE MANSION
CHAPTER ONE

THE ONLY THING Annabelle didn't like about driving her royal blue Mini Cooper was that when she did so, she couldn't see how pretty it looked against the lush English countryside. In her mind, the various green hues of the fields, trees, and hedgerows provided the perfect backdrop for her petite, blue bullet of a car as it raced around the country lanes. She would picture herself zooming along like a character in a lavishly produced television drama with an audience of millions, a happy ending guaranteed.

Annabelle loved driving. She loved driving almost as much as she loved cake, and that was saying something. Annabelle's enthusiasm for sugary treats was as well-known in the village of Upton St. Mary as her easy-going yet stead-fast character. She was coming up to her third year as vicar of the small, close-knit parish, yet the countryside that surrounded it, with its elegantly built stone walls, undu-lating landscape of green hills, and ancient trees, still took her breath away. As she whipped the terrier-like motor along the country lanes of the Cornish countryside, she found it impossible not to smile. Going for a spin in her

Mini with its go-faster stripes, followed by a cup of tea and a slice of cake was Annabelle's idea of a perfect summer's afternoon.

Annabelle had grown up among the hustle and bustle of working-class London, daughter of a street-savvy cabbie and a friendly, hard-working cleaning lady, but she had always dreamed of finding a peaceful, serene idyll where she might settle. A place filled with beauty, calm, and goodness. Annabelle's soul had found it in the glow of the Lord, and her body found it in this quaint little village tucked into a beautiful corner at the very end of England. Even the frequent rains and chilly winters couldn't spoil this very British garden of Eden for her.

The villagers, many of whom had spent their entire lives there, were just as appreciative of Upton St. Mary as their entranced vicar. Many of their pastimes and traditions involved enjoying the company of their good-natured neighbours and their delightfully well-maintained cottages. Locals also loved nothing more than a crafts fair or some other competition in which they could display their talents for gardening, knitting, pottery, and—frequently to Annabelle's delight—baking.

The villagers were very proud of Upton St. Mary, and retaining its rustic charm attracted much attention. A lot of energy attended every local issue. Whether it was a problematic pothole or a controversial building extension, the villagers held very strong opinions, which they voiced at every opportunity.

The strictly-held conventions of the village, coupled with the speed at which gossip travelled through the community, meant that Annabelle's introduction as the new vicar had been greeted with reluctance by some, and concern by others. "A female vicar? In Upton St. Mary?

What on earth will we do?" said one particularly anxious voice. "It's a slippery slope. Today a female vicar, tomorrow there'll be a coffee bar where the tea shop used to be!" said another.

But Annabelle was not the type to be fazed. Her dedication to church matters was unparalleled. With an abundance of enthusiasm, she delivered sermons with devotion and strokes of well-appointed humour whilst galvanising more than a few reticent churchgoers to attend services more often than ever before. She was never too busy to lend a hand here or an ear there. She didn't hesitate to put on her wellies and get stuck in with the farmers. She would stop to chat with the ladies in the tea shop, navigating their discussions with decorum and grace. She quickly became the presence villagers wanted at their bedside when ill and their first port of call when a dispute needed resolving fairly and with tact. In sum, Annabelle was irresistible.

Her predecessor had been male, a distinctly hairy male, and relations had been all quite straightforward. However, Annabelle's appointment had put the villagers in a quandary. How should they address their new female priest? Was her gender to be a cause for impropriety and social faux-pas? "Father" had long been the accepted term, and now that was out of the question. Much discussion ensued on the subject until Annabelle put an end to it with decisiveness and sensibility. The villagers were to call her "Vicar," "Reverend," or just plain "Annabelle." With their concerns allayed, everyone went on their merry way.

Yes, Annabelle had become a widely accepted and to many, a much-loved boon to the village. The fact that her clerical collar was wrapped around a distinctly feminine, and surprisingly elegant neck had now been forgotten (or at least ignored) by those who were perhaps a little slower to embrace the new ways of the world. With good humour and grace, she had settled into the gentle, quiet pace of life a village church position afforded and, in the process, made it easy for the villagers to love her.

As Annabelle eased her Mini along Upton St. Mary's tightly woven, cobblestone streets, she waved at Mr. Hawthorne as he passed by on his bicycle. He was a mischievous man of sixty who told tall tales of his youth. And whilst he claimed to ride his bike every morning "for the constitutional benefits," it was an open secret in the village that he rode to a secluded spot where he could enjoy the pleasure of his pipe away from the prying eyes and sensitive nose of his disapproving wife.

Annabelle reached a small house on the outskirts, as cute and prim as she knew its owner to be. She stopped the car and got out. The sun was just beginning to sprinkle dappled yellow light across the rooftops. Annabelle took a deep breath of crisp, fresh air. She detected a faint whiff of something sweet and warm. She briskly locked the car door, marched to the front of the house, and knocked cheerily.

After a few moments, the door opened the tiniest of slivers revealing a pair of deep blue eyes and not much else. "Good morning, Annabelle," said an elderly woman before she opened the door wider and quickly hurried further back into the house.

"Good morning, Philippa," said Annabelle, wiping her feet on the doormat and following her through the cottage. "Why do you insist on opening the door in that manner? I feel like a door-to-door salesman. I'm sure you're not expecting anyone else at this hour."

"Better safe than sorry," said Philippa, leading the way past a paper-strewn desk and into the kitchen.

"Oh, these look scrumptious!" squealed Annabelle,

catching sight of the range of cakes Philippa had laid on the kitchen table.

Philippa smiled, took the teapot, and began pouring tea.

"I'm trying something new this year. I might experiment with nuts a little. Walnuts, almonds, that sort of thing. I thought it might give me a better chance of standing out at the fair."

"Mmm," mumbled Annabelle, already munching on a particularly rich and utterly delicious cupcake, her ravenous appetite winning the battle over ladylike reserve. "Your baking always stands out, Philippa."

"Thank you, Annabelle," Philippa chuckled, "but there's some stiff competition in Upton St. Mary. I even considered baklava at one point."

"Baklava? I haven't the foggiest idea what that might be."

"It reminds me of my youth and a trip I took to Greece. You'd love baklava. It's a sweet pastry drenched in honey and nuts. *Very* continental." Philippa winked.

"Well, I say jolly well go for it!" Annabelle exclaimed, putting down the cake and sipping at her tea.

"Oh, I couldn't, Annabelle."

"Why ever not?"

"Think of the outrage!"

Annabelle considered the point for a moment before nodding. Upton St. Mary welcomed new people but was not nearly as benevolent to new ideas.

To get your copy of Murder at the Mansion visit the link below:
https://www.alisongolden.com/murder-at-the-mansion

REVERENTIAL RECIPES

Continue on to check
out the recipes for
goodies featured in
this book...

CHERISHABLE CHERRY BLOSSOM CUPCAKES

For the cupcakes
1 stick (115g) butter
4 egg whites
2 cups (240g) flour
1 ½ teaspoons baking powder
½ teaspoon salt
¾ cup (180ml) whole milk
⅓ cup (80ml) maraschino cherry juice
1 ¾ cups (350g) sugar
1 teaspoon vanilla extract
½ teaspoon almond extract
Maraschino cherries with stems
(decoration)

For the frosting
1 cup (230g) butter, softened
4 cups (480g) icing sugar
3 tablespoons maraschino cherry juice
½ teaspoon almond extract

Preheat the oven to 180°C/350°F/Gas Mark 4. Line cupcake tins with paper liners. Allow butter and egg whites to stand at room temperature for 30 minutes.

In a medium bowl, sift together flour, baking powder, and salt. In a separate bowl, whisk together the milk and cherry juice until combined. In a large mixing bowl, beat butter with an electric mixer on medium to high speed for 30 seconds.

Add sugar, vanilla and almond extracts to the butter. Beat until combined. Add egg whites, one at a time, beating well after each addition. Alternately, add flour mixture and milk mixture beating on low speed until just combined. Spoon mixture into each paper liner, filling them about ⅔ full.

Bake the cupcakes until a toothpick inserted into the centre comes out clean, about 20 to 25 minutes. Leave to cool completely.

To make the frosting, in a large mixing bowl beat butter until smooth. Gradually add two cups of the icing sugar, beating well. Gradually beat in ⅔ of the maraschino cherry juice and all of the almond extract. Beat in the additional icing sugar slowly. If necessary, add the additional juice one teaspoon at a time until icing reaches a spreadable consistency. Top cupcakes with frosting and add whole cherries for decoration.

Makes approximately 24 cupcakes.

CHERUBIC CHOCOLATE CARAMEL BARS

For the base
5 oz (140g) butter
½ cup (100g) sugar
1 ¼ cups (150g) flour
4 oz (115g) dark chocolate, broken into
pieces, for topping

For the filling
½ cup (115g) butter
½ cup (100g) sugar
2 tablespoons Lyles golden syrup
14 oz (400g) can condensed milk

Preheat the oven to 180°C/350°F/Gas Mark 4. Grease a 30cm x 22.5cm/12 x 9 inch oven tray/flat baking tray and dust with flour.

To prepare the base, cream the butter and sugar together in a mixing bowl. Work in the flour with a wooden spoon or electric mixer. Press into the baking tray and bake for 15 to 20 minutes or until shortbread base is golden in colour. Remove from the oven and leave to cool.

To prepare the filling, put all the ingredients in a pan and heat gently until the sugar has dissolved, stirring occasionally. Increase the heat and, taking care not to burn, boil the mixture slowly for 5 minutes, stirring continuously. Remove from the heat, leave to cool for 1 minute, then pour onto the cooled shortbread base. Leave to set.

Melt the chocolate in a small heatproof bowl over a pan of hot water. Spread over the set filling. Mark into portions, fingers or squares, and leave until quite cold and set before removing from the baking tray.

Makes 18-20.

JUBILICIOUS JAM TURNOVERS

For the pastry
8 oz (230g) flour
¼ teaspoon salt
1 ¼ stick butter
1 oz (30g) lard
½ cup (120ml) cold water

For the filling
Approximately 1 1/2 cups (340g) strawberry or apricot jam

To finish
Milk
Sugar

Sift the flour and salt into a mixing bowl. Add the butter and lard in walnut-sized pieces, and rub into the flour. Add water a teaspoon at a time until you can press the dough gently together with floured hands. Roll out on a well-floured board into a long thin oblong shape with a floured rolling-pin, keeping the edges as straight as possible with a palette knife.

Fold this oblong strip into three with the open edge facing you. Turn the dough a quarter of a turn clock-wise, and roll out to an oblong shape again. Repeat this folding and rolling process three more times, turning the dough a quarter of a turn each time it is folded. Fold into three, wrap in cling wrap and chill in the refrigerator for 30 minutes.

Preheat the oven to 200°C/400°F/Gas Mark 6. Line two oven trays with baking paper. Roll out the chilled dough very thinly into a square shape. Cut into 12 x 10 cm/4 inch squares. Put two teaspoons of jam just off centre on each square of dough, leaving a margin. Dampen the edges with water. Fold the dough over the jam to form a triangular shape and press the edges together to seal. Brush with a little milk and dredge with sugar.

Place on over tray. Bake in the oven for 15-20 minutes or until the pastry is puffed and golden-brown. Keep an eye on them as they cook quickly.

Makes approximately 12 turnovers.

TERESA'S SURPRISE CAKE

For the cake
1 ¾ cups (210g) flour
1 teaspoon baking powder
¾ teaspoon baking soda
¼ teaspoon salt
1 stick (115g) unsalted butter, softened
1⅓ cups (265g) extra-fine sugar
1 ¾ oz (50g) unsweetened cocoa powder
1 teaspoon almond extract
2 large eggs
2 oz (55g) unsweetened chocolate, melted
½ cup (120ml) water
½ cup (120ml) milk

For the frosting
1 ¼ cups (300g) heavy whipping cream
1 stick (115g) softened unsalted butter
1 tsp almond flavouring
¼ cup (30g) icing sugar

For the mousse

8 oz (225g) semi-sweet chocolate
1 stick (115g) unsalted butter
2/3 cup (160g) heavy whipping cream
4 large eggs
6 tbsp extra-fine sugar
2 tbsp water

For the ganache

4 oz (115g) chopped semi-sweet chocolate
½ cup (120g) heavy cream
3 tbsp light corn syrup
1 tbsp palm shortening
½ tsp almond flavouring

For decoration

2 tbsp slivered almonds

Preheat oven to 160°C/325°F/Gas Mark 3 and position rack in the centre of the oven. Prepare a 22.5 cm/9 inch round cake tin by lining the bottom and sides with baking paper and brushing lightly with oil. Melt the chocolate in a small heatproof bowl over a pan of hot water. Allow to cool slightly. Sift the flour, baking powder, baking soda, and salt together in a bowl and set aside until ready to use.

In a large mixing bowl, cream butter, then add sugar, almond flavouring and cocoa powder with an electric mixer until well blended. The appearance will be grainy and lumpy. Gradually add eggs, one at a time, mixing until each is incorporated into the mixture. Add melted chocolate to creamed mixture and blend it in so that the batter is smooth.

Heat the milk with the water until hot to touch (not boiling). Set aside. Add the dry ingredients to the mixing bowl with the butter, sugar, chocolate mixture. Slowly fold in, then mix until completely blended. With your electric mixer on slow, pour in the hot milk and water. Increase the speed to medium to completely mix everything together. If it is too stiff, add water a tablespoon at a time to get a soft but not loose cake batter consistency.

Pour the batter into the prepared cake tin and place in the preheated oven for 40 minutes, or until a wooden tooth-pick inserted into the centre comes out clean. Allow to cool completely before removing it from the cake tin. Once cooled, wrap the cake with plastic wrap and place in the fridge until completely chilled (about 1 ½ hours).

While the cake is cooling, prepare the chocolate mousse. Melt the chocolate and butter together in a small heatproof bowl over a pan of hot water. When the mixture is completely smooth and glossy, scrape into a large bowl and set aside.

In a clean bowl, mix the heavy cream until it comes together and whip lines are slightly visible. Place in the fridge to keep chilled.

Heat eggs, sugar, and water in a small heatproof bowl over a pan of hot water. Whip until frothy, and warm to the touch. Pour the mixture into a clean bowl and mix on high until the mixture is very thick, smooth, and nearly white in colour, about 8-12 minutes.

Scoop about ⅓ of the egg mixture into the melted chocolate and butter, and using a folding motion, lightly blend. There will be streaks of light and dark in the mixture. Add the rest of the egg mixture to the chocolate, carefully folding until a fairly uniform tone. Lightly fold in whipped cream. Place the mousse in the fridge until it is solid and the cake is ready to assemble.

To assemble the cake, very lightly spray a 22.5 cm/9

inch springform tin with oil and line it with baking paper. Remove the cake from the refrigerator and using a very long, sharp knife, slowly slice through its middle to create two layers of equal size. (A serrated, sharp, bread-knife works well).

Carefully place one layer into the bottom of the spring-form tin making sure it is snug. Remove the mousse from the fridge and spread half of it over the cake layer, making sure to even it out to the edges. Add the second layer of cake and place it over the mousse. Gently press.

Spread the remaining mousse over the second cake layer, spreading to smooth it out on top. Place the cake in the freezer for at least 4 hours. If you are making this one day in advance, once the top of the cake is firm to touch, cover it in plastic wrap.

While cake is chilling, prepare almond buttercream frosting. In a bowl, beat the heavy whipping cream until holds its shape in peaks, chill. In a separate clean bowl, cream softened butter, icing sugar, and almond flavouring until smooth. Combine the chilled cream into the almond buttercream mixture. Chill until ready to use (at least 1 ½ hours).

Once the cake and mousse layers are chilled, the cake is ready to be frosted. Prepare the cake plate you will serve the cake on by lining it with pieces of baking paper to be removed after icing. Remove the springform tin from the freezer.

Run a thin knife smoothly around the edge of the pan to help release it. Remove the cake from the tin and peel off the baking paper from its bottom. Place the cake on the prepared cake plate. Spread the top and sides thinly with the chilled almond buttercream frosting. Place in the refrigerator while the chocolate ganache and decoration are prepared.

To make the ganache topping, heat the heavy cream, corn syrup, and palm shortening in a pan until just below boiling. Stir to blend, then pour the mixture over the chopped chocolate. Allow to sit for two minutes, then mix well until everything is smooth and glossy. Add the almond flavouring and stir well.

To use immediately, remove the cake from the refrigerator, pour the ganache over the surface of the cake and with an offset spatula, quickly smooth across the surface of the cake, allowing some to dribble down the sides. Place the cake back in the refrigerator.

If making the ganache ahead of time, place in the refrigerator in a covered container. When ready to use, heat in a microwave to bring to a pourable consistency and proceed as described above.

To prepare the toasted almond decoration, place almond slivers in a heavy, ungreased skillet. Stir continuously over medium heat until golden brown. Cool for 30-40 minutes.

Remove the cake and put the toasted almond slivers along the edge of the finished cake, pressing in gently. This decoration gives the cake a delightful finish and elegant, nutty flavour.

Notes

It is suggested that, for best results, this cake is made a day prior to serving, otherwise, allow at least six hours to make and assemble cake. Make sure the cake has ample time, at least 30 minutes, in the refrigerator to thaw before serving. Use a warm knife to slice through.

Serves 16-20.

All ingredients are available from your local store or online retailer.

You can find printable versions of these recipes at www.alisongolden.com/dcrecipes

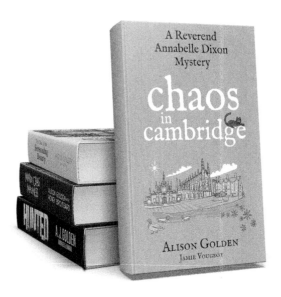

"Your emails seem to come on days when I need to read them because they are so upbeat."
- Linda W -

For a limited time, you can get the first books in each of my series - *Chaos in Cambridge, Hunted* (exclusively for subscribers - not available anywhere else), *The Case of the Screaming Beauty, and Mardi Gras Madness* - plus updates about new releases, promotions, and other Insider exclusives, by signing up for my mailing list at:

https://www.alisongolden.com/annabelle

TAKE MY QUIZ

What kind of mystery reader are you? Take my thirty second quiz to find out!

https://www.alisongolden.com/quiz

BOOKS IN THE REVEREND ANNABELLE DIXON SERIES

Chaos in Cambridge (Prequel)

Death at the Café

Murder at the Mansion

Body in the Woods

Grave in the Garage

Horror in the Highlands

Killer at the Cult

Fireworks in France

Witches at the Wedding

COLLECTIONS

Books 1-4

Death at the Café

Murder at the Mansion

Body in the Woods

Grave in the Garage

Books 5-7

Horror in the Highlands

Killer at the Cult

Fireworks in France

Snatched

Stolen

Chopped

Exposed

ABOUT THE AUTHOR

Alison Golden is the *USA Today* bestselling author of the Inspector David Graham mysteries, a traditional British detective series, and two cozy mystery series featuring main characters Reverend Annabelle Dixon and Roxy Reinhardt. As A. J. Golden, she writes the Diana Hunter thriller series.

Alison was raised in Bedfordshire, England. Her aim is to write stories that are designed to entertain, amuse, and calm. Her approach is to combine creative ideas with excellent writing and edit, edit, edit. Alison's mission is simple: To write excellent books that have readers clamouring for more.

Alison is based in the San Francisco Bay Area with her husband and twin sons. She splits her time between London and San Francisco.

For up-to-date promotions and release dates of upcoming books, sign up for the latest news here: https:// alisongolden.com/annabelle.

For more information:
www.alisongolden.com
alison@alisongolden.com

facebook.com/alisongolden.books

twitter.com/alisonjgolden

instagram.com/alisonjgolden

THANK YOU

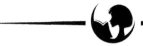

Thank you for taking the time to read *Death at the Café*. If you enjoyed it, please consider telling your friends or posting a short review. Word of mouth is an author's best friend and very much appreciated.

Thank you,

Printed in Great Britain
by Amazon

57425707R00101